The Power of Inner Strength

Building Mental Toughness in Young Athletes

Jack Laforet

© Copyright 2024 - All rights reserved.

The content contained within this book may not be reproduced, duplicated or transmitted without direct written permission from the author or the publisher.

Under no circumstances will any blame or legal responsibility be held against the publisher, or author, for any damages, reparation, or monetary loss due to the information contained within this book, either directly or indirectly.

Legal Notice:

This book is copyright protected. It is only for personal use. You cannot amend, distribute, sell, use, quote or paraphrase any part, or the content within this book, without the consent of the author or publisher.

Disclaimer Notice:

Please note the information contained within this document is for educational and entertainment purposes only. All effort has been executed to present accurate, up to date, reliable, complete information. No warranties of any kind are declared or implied. Readers acknowledge that the author is not engaged in the rendering of legal, financial, medical or professional advice. The content within this book has been derived from various sources. Please consult a licensed professional before attempting any techniques outlined in this book.

By reading this document, the reader agrees that under no circumstances is the author responsible for any losses, direct or indirect, that are incurred as a result of the use of the information contained within this document, including, but not limited to, errors, omissions, or inaccuracies.

Table of Contents

YOU GOT THIS! 1
    TAKING THE FIRST STEP 1
        An Emotional, Mental, and Physical Roller Coaster 2

CHAPTER 1: UNLEASHING YOUR INNER STRENGTH 5
    THE POWER WITHIN—WHAT IS MENTAL TOUGHNESS? 5
        Mental Toughness in Everyday Life 7
        The 4 C's of Mental Toughness 7
        How Does Mental Toughness Impact Gameplay? 10
    BREAKING DOWN THE BARRIERS 11
        Common Barriers to Mental Toughness 11
        Myth or Fact? 12
    QUIZ TIME— HOW IS YOUR MENTAL TOUGHNESS? 13

CHAPTER 2: THE PARENT/COACH PLAYBOOK 15
    COACHING FOR MENTAL STRENGTH 15
        The Role of a Coach 16
        Do's and Don'ts of Coaching 19
    PARENTS AS PILLARS OF SUPPORT 20
        The Role of the Parent to Athletes 21
        The Role of the Parent to Athletes 22
        Finding the Balance 23
        How to Give Support On and Off the Field 24
    A WINNING COMBINATION—THE PARENT COACH DUO 26
    QUIZ TIME 27
        Coaches: What's Your Coaching Style? 27
        Parents: What's Your Communication Style? 29

CHAPTER 3: DREAM BIG— GOAL SETTING AND MOTIVATION 33
    FROM VISION TO REALITY—SETTING GOALS 33
        Why Set Goals? 34
        How to Set Goals 34
        SMART Goals 35
        Linking Values and Our Athletic Goals 36
    FUELING OUR FIRE 37
        Finding Motivation Amongst Frustration 37
        Common Obstacles Athletes Face 38
        Intrinsic vs. Extrinsic Motivation 39
        Staying Motivated and Positive 40

    TEMPLATE—GOAL SETTING 41
    QUIZ TIME: WHAT'S YOUR MOTIVATION? 42

CHAPTER 4: THE KEY TO SUCCESS: CONFIDENCE 45

    BUILDING THE FOUNDATION? 45
        Where Does My Confidence Come From? *45*
    HITTING BACK AT SELF-DOUBT 47
        Why Do We Struggle to Embrace Success? *48*
        Not All Failures Are Bad *48*
    FUELED BY NAYSAYERS 50
        Handling Criticism—the Good and the Bad *51*
    QUIZ TIME: HOW'S YOUR CONFIDENCE? 52

CHAPTER 5: THE POWER OF FOCUS AND CONCENTRATION 55

    FINDING YOUR FOCUS 55
        How Does Focus and Concentration Impact Gameplay? *56*
    BLOCKING OUT DISTRACTIONS 57
        Why Do We Make Excuses? *58*
        Managing Distractions and Excuses *58*
    MENTALLY PREPARING AND TRAINING OUR MIND 59
        Coping With Pressures *59*
        Techniques to Cope With Pressure *60*
    QUIZ TIME: AM I EASILY DISTRACTED? 61

CHAPTER 6: MASTERING STRESS AND PRESSURE 65

        Stresses Athletes Face *66*
        Recognizing the Signs of Stress *66*
    DEMYSTIFYING STRESS AND PRESSURE IN SPORTS 67
        Destressing Techniques *68*
    TIME MANAGEMENT AND STRESS 69
        Resilience in Stress and Pressure *70*
        Knowing Your Boundaries and Limits *70*
        Rest *71*
        Recovery *71*
        Self-Care *71*
    TEN QUICK TIPS FOR 72
        Stress-Busting *72*
        Pressure Mantras *73*

CHAPTER 7: THE RESILIENT ATHLETE 75

    WHAT MAKES A RESILIENT ATHLETE 76
        How Does Resilience Play Into Sports? *77*
    ACHIEVING A RESILIENT MINDSET 79
        Characteristics of a Resilient Athlete *79*

Quiz Time: Am I Resilient? 81

CHAPTER 8: TEAMWORK: HOW TO THRIVE AS A TEAM PLAYER 85

There's No "I" in Team 85
    Teamwork Makes the Dream Work... 86
Becoming a Leader On and Off the Field 88
    Balancing Leadership With Individuality 88
Navigating Conflict... 89
    Common Conflicts in Sports and Team Play 89
    Conflict Resolution Techniques 90
Quiz Time: Am I a Team Player? 91

CHAPTER 9: THE BALANCING ACT: SCHOOL, LIFE AND SPORTS 93

Juggling Our Many Hats 93
    The Struggle to Embracing Multiple Identities 94
    Wearing Your Hat With Pride 95
How to Balance Sports and Life 95
    Ways to Create Balance.. 96
    Don't Forget Self-Care 97
Balancing Relationships 98
    Balancing Teammates and Friendships 98
    Creating a Circle of Support and Encouragement 98

CONCLUSION: THE ROAD AHEAD 101

Following Your Passion 101

REFERENCES..103

You Got This!

Success is a journey, not a destination. The doing is often more important than the outcome. –Arthur Ashe

Taking the First Step

Embarking on a journey of self-improvement and mental strength starts with the powerful and courageous decision to recognize and acknowledge one's weaknesses. This simple yet sometimes daunting act is not a sign of defeat; it is the first step towards becoming the best version of yourself. It takes immense courage to admit to yourself that there is room to grow and uncover new heights of greatness and success that you may not even know you possess. This sometimes-undervalued act of courage and humility demonstrates one's commitment towards personal development and one's desire to grow continually—mentally, emotionally, and physically.

This journey you are about to embark on will not be easy. There will be challenges, setbacks and moments of self-doubt. You may encounter days where it feels like the losses outnumber the wins. Yet, this is where mental strength is tested. As athletes, one understands the endless and sometimes extensive training and dedication needed to compete at the highest levels and against the world's best. At the same time, it will also require athletes to ensure they have the foundation and the ability to demonstrate mental resilience by enduring and overcoming whatever barriers and obstacles come their way. The road ahead will be long, but if you have unwavering persistence and dedication, you can and will transform these challenges into stepping stones toward your success.

An Emotional, Mental, and Physical Roller Coaster

Consider some of the biggest names in sports, household names and athletes who have faced great adversity and yet have emerged as champions.

Kobe Bryant is often considered one of the greatest basketball players of all time. He was known for his relentless work ethic and "Mamba Mentality." Bryant (2018) once said, "Everything negative—challenges—are all an opportunity for me to rise." Bryant's unwavering commitment to excellence, even in the face of setbacks, is a testament to the power of perseverance.

Similarly, Tiger Woods, one of golf's most iconic figures, has faced personal and professional challenges that would have ended the careers of many other athletes; however, Woods' belief in continuous improvement, along with his mantra of "winning takes care of everything" (Wismer, 2013) put him back at the top of tournaments and in the limelight. Woods' journey underscores the importance of resilience, the ability to bounce back, and the strength to keep moving forward even when things seem and feel impossible.

These are just two athletes, amongst many others, who did not become great by avoiding challenges or allowing the roller coaster of greatness to hold them back. They embraced the journey to the top and recognized that every setback was an opportunity to learn, grow, and improve. Their stories and journey are powerful reminders that mental strength is not a gift but rather a skill developed through experience, effort, and persistence.

As you begin your journey towards mental resilience and strength, remember that it's not about being perfect but about making progress. Each step you take, no matter how small, is a step closer to the person you strive to be. Embrace the process, learn from failing, and trust that with each challenge you overcome, you will become stronger and more prepared for what lies ahead.

This book explores principles and practices that can help you develop the mental courage to face the obstacles to becoming a great athlete. Examine your experiences, habits, and mentality as you gain the tools and insights to improve mentally, emotionally, and physically. The journey may be challenging, but it is one worth taking if you want to become and do more.

Remember, every great achievement starts with taking the first step.

Chapter 1:

Unleashing Your Inner Strength

Strength does not come from winning. Your struggles develop your strengths. When you go through hardships and decide not to surrender, that is strength.

–Arnold Schwarzenegger

The Power Within—What Is Mental Toughness?

You may have heard sayings such as "mind over matter" or "shift your mindset"—these are just a few examples of phrases meant to promote or encourage mental toughness.

But what is mental toughness? Mental toughness is an umbrella term that touches on success, resilience, and high performance. It's the psychological edge that enables athletes (predominantly) to remain focused, determined, and resilient in moments of adversity. That inner strength allows one to push through challenges while maintaining composure under pressure, ultimately resulting in them achieving their goals.

But don't be fooled; just because it's "mental" does not mean it is only about being tough on the inside. It's also about being emotionally resilient. It involves a combination of perseverance, self-belief, and the ability to manage one's emotions, which can be difficult under stress and pressure. Think about a time when you found yourself acting out of emotion and not using logic. It's when we act out and don't think things through that mistakes can happen.

Unlike physical toughness, which is visible and measurable, mental toughness is internal. It is a mindset that is developed and strengthened over time. However, just as it can be strengthened, there are times when we can find ourselves falling back into bad habits of frustration and discouragement.

Why Does Mental Toughness Matter?

Have you asked yourself this question before? Not an easy question, is it?

The answer to this question lies in how we respond to the inevitable challenges and obstacles we encounter in life—both as athletes and non-athletes.

Why?

Challenges are a part of everyday life, even when we do not want them to be. How we deal with these challenges often determines our level of success and resilience. Mental toughness equips us with the ability to navigate these problems while not losing focus on the end goal.

It is because of this that mental toughness matters because it influences every aspect of our lives; it affects how we approach each problem and stressor we encounter ("Mental Toughness," 2021). By recognizing and preparing for the challenges in our lives, we are training our minds to know how to remain calm under pressure and stress. As athletes, remaining cool, calm, and collected can be crucial in those final moments where every second and every action matters.

Do you really want to find yourself choking on that layup? Or do you want to lose focus as you are about to take your final swing on the last hole?

No, you do not, and that is why mental toughness matters. Mental toughness separates the athletes pushing forward from those who concede to the challenges and walk away. Be the athlete who strives to be the best 100% of the time, and not 50%.

Mental Toughness in Everyday Life

When it comes to mentally training ourselves to be mentally tough, this does not just apply to the athlete hat you wear—it applies to all aspects of your life. Having mental toughness in everyday life can lead to this sense of accomplishment and fulfillment. Whether you are facing challenges at school or work, or maybe you are dealing with personal setbacks—regardless of what you are facing, mental toughness helps remind you of what you are working toward. It reminds you that hard work is much more rewarding than taking the easy route.

Take, for example, mentally tough individuals in the workplace who can work in high-pressure situations. Those who can handle these situations often do so with grace and confidence. They can also take constructive criticism and learn from their mistakes while continuing to grow and develop.

In personal relationships, mental toughness allows individuals to navigate conflicts with empathy and understanding rather than reacting impulsively or emotionally, not that there is anything wrong with emotions.

Mental toughness can profoundly impact one's mental health and well-being. Given that it can touch every aspect of one's life, it is important to know how to deal with the pressures and stressors of life—on and off the field. Demonstrating mental toughness can remind us of our purpose, our goals, and our aspirations.

While this chapter and much of the book examine mental toughness through the lens of an athlete, it's important to remember that it is an invaluable skill for anyone who wants to live a life with purpose, confidence, and assurance.

The 4 C's of Mental Toughness

We have discussed the importance and value of mental toughness in our everyday lives, and now, it is important to understand its four key components.

Often referred to as the 4 C's: Control, Commitment, Challenge, and Confidence, each plays a crucial role in developing and maintaining mental toughness on and off the field.

Control

Control is about managing one's emotions, maintaining composure under pressure, and not allowing external factors (things beyond one's ability) to dictate their actions or reactions.

This important component of mental toughness helps individuals stay focused and composed, even in challenging and pressured situations. It is also important to note that mental toughness sometimes involves letting go of control, just as much as it is about having control. For instance, in situations where outcomes are beyond our influence, mental toughness means accepting the results and adapting accordingly. We may not like it, but if we can pivot and take what comes our way— we will be better off mentally and emotionally.

An example of control could be an athlete staying calm and focused during a crucial moment in a game or a competitor maintaining composure during a high-pressure race. On the flip side, a lack of control might be seen as a player who lets their emotions take over, leading to poor decision-making during a critical moment in the competition or recklessness on the court, resulting in the injury of either them or other players.

Commitment

Commitment refers to setting and focusing on achieving goals. It's about discipline, staying the course, and not giving up in the face of adversity.

Commitment is essential to mental toughness because it drives athletes to keep going, even when the journey becomes difficult. Without commitment, it's easy to lose sight of long-term goals, get discouraged by setbacks, or abandon efforts when results are not immediate.

For example, a committed basketball player might practice tirelessly daily, pushing through fatigue and minor injuries to improve their skills. On the other hand, a lack of commitment might be seen as an athlete who skips practice, makes excuses, or gives up quickly when faced with tough competition or when they are losing.

Challenge

Challenge is another key aspect of mental toughness. It is not just about overcoming difficulties but seeing them as opportunities for growth and stepping stones toward becoming a stronger, more resilient athlete. It's about embracing obstacles as a natural part of the process, knowing that each one you conquer makes you better, stronger, and more prepared for the next.

They are the litmus test of an athlete's mental toughness. They push you out of your comfort zone, forcing you to adapt, learn, and grow. However, it's important to have a balance to the amount of challenge one faces. Being overly challenged can result in burnout, and too little can result in complacency. At the end of the day, you want to find that sweet spot where you are challenged just enough that you are driven to move forward and upward but not too much that you become frustrated and discouraged.

An example of a challenge might be a tennis player who adjusts their strategy and mindset after losing the first set to return and win the match.

Confidence

Confidence is the assurance that you can achieve your goals, no matter the challenges. This mental toughness component fuels persistence and willingness to take risks. With confidence, you can face challenges head-on, knowing that you have what it takes to succeed.

If athletes lack confidence, they may be hesitant or reluctant, or they may even doubt themselves. They avoid situations where they think they may not come out victorious.

An example of confidence might be a gymnast attempting a difficult routine for the first time; if they are confident, they will have trust in all the training they have done, as well as their skills and capability. If they do not, they may make a mistake or psych themselves out.

How Does Mental Toughness Impact Gameplay?

Whether or not an athlete is aware of it, mental toughness is a key determinant of their success and failure, especially in high-pressure situations. Demonstrating mental toughness is about maintaining composure when and where it matters most.

Here are a few ways mental toughness impacts gameplay:

Performing Under Pressure:

Having mental toughness empowers athletes to excel under pressure. It's the invisible force behind a basketball player's game-deciding free throw. It instills this mindset of trust in their training, which decreases the likelihood of experiencing performance anxiety.

Recovering from Mistakes:

Athletes with mental toughness move on quickly from mistakes. Mistakes are inevitable, but successful athletes bounce back immediately. For example, a tennis player who double-faults during a crucial moment learns from the mistake and shifts her mindset to stay focused on the present moment rather than dwelling on the past. When one dwells on a mistake, it can result in a loss of confidence and increased self-doubt, ultimately impacting their performance.

Consistency in Performance:

Mental toughness helps athletes maintain consistent performance over time. Mental endurance, whether pacing through a long race or staying sharp throughout a season, is crucial. Not having a consistent mindset (whether training or competing), athletes may experience burnout.

Developing mental toughness is not just about improving one's athletic ability; it's about cultivating the right mindset needed to perform at the highest possible level, day in and day out.

Breaking Down the Barriers

While we would like to believe that mental toughness can happen overnight, it unfortunately does not. Rather, it requires consistent effort and the continual ability to overcome the barriers that athletes experience regularly.

Common Barriers to Mental Toughness

Here are some common barriers that athletes experience:

Performance Anxiety: Being nervous can impact performance, resulting in physical symptoms like increased heart rate and tension. This is particularly challenging for younger or less experienced athletes or athletes competing on a larger scale.

Self-Doubt: Athletes who question their abilities may hesitate, leading them to underperform. Overcoming self-doubt involves trusting in one's ability, training and positive reinforcement by focusing on past successes.

Fear of Failure: While a perfectionist mindset may be good in theory, it can prevent athletes from taking risks and limit growth. Embracing challenges and learning from setbacks is crucial to overcoming this fear.

Negative Self-Talk: Phrases like "I'm not good enough" undermine one's confidence and motivation. Replacing negative thoughts with positive affirmations helps build resilience. Statements such as "I can do this" or "This is what you've been training for" can change the negative to positive.

Lack of Focus: One of the biggest barriers is losing focus, especially when there are barriers or distractions; therefore, learning to tune out these distractions can help maintain that focus.

Myth or Fact?

As athletes, we often rely on those around us to help us reach our peak; however, sometimes, the shared information can be a bit inaccurate or misleading.

How well do you know what myth or fact is when it comes to mental toughness?

Myth: Mental toughness means never showing emotion.

Fact: It's about managing emotions effectively, not suppressing them.

Myth: Only elite athletes possess it.

Fact: It can be developed by anyone through practice and dedication.

Myth: You're either born with it or not.

Fact: It's a skill that can be cultivated over time.

Myth: Strong athletes don't need help.

Fact: Support from coaches, teammates, or professionals benefits everyone.

Myth: Physical appearance indicates toughness.

Fact: Resilience is about inner qualities like determination and focus, not physical looks.

Quiz Time—
How Is Your Mental Toughness?

Take this quiz to see how mentally tough you are.

1. When faced with a challenging situation, you are most likely to:

    a. Give up easily
    b. Feel overwhelmed, but try to push through
    c. Embrace the challenge and look for solutions

1. How do you handle criticism?

    a. Take it personally and feel discouraged
    b. Reflect on it and try to improve
    c. Use it as motivation to do better

2. In a high-pressure situation, you typically:

    a. Panic and make hasty decisions
    b. Feel stressed but try to stay focused
    c. Remain calm and think clearly

3. When you experience failure, you:

    a. Blame external factors
    b. Feel disappointed but move on
    c. Analyze what went wrong and learn from it

4. How do you set goals for yourself?

    a. Rarely set goals
    b. Set goals but sometimes lack a clear plan
    c. Set specific, achievable goals with a clear action plan

5. How do you handle unexpected changes or setbacks?

    a. Get frustrated and lose motivation
    b. Try to adapt but struggle with it
    c. Stay flexible and look for new opportunities

6. When working towards a long-term goal, you:

    a. Often lose interest and give up
    b. Maintain effort but sometimes lose focus
    c. Stay dedicated and consistently work towards it

7. How do you maintain your focus and motivation over time?

    a. Find it difficult to stay motivated
    b. Use occasional reminders to stay on track
    c. Regularly review and adjust your plans to stay motivated

Breaking Down Your Results:

Mostly A's: You might struggle with mental toughness in challenging situations. Consider working on strategies to build resilience and coping skills.

Mostly B's: You have a moderate level of mental toughness. You can handle stress and challenges but might benefit from strengthening your mindset further.

Mostly C's: You demonstrate strong mental toughness. You handle challenges well, stay focused on your goals, and use setbacks as opportunities to grow.

Chapter 2:

The Parent/Coach Playbook

The will to prepare has to be greater than the will to win. –Bobby Knight

Coaching for Mental Strength

When it comes to coaching for mental strength, a coach's role is to guide the athlete toward developing the necessary psychological resilience, self-confidence, and emotional regulation required for their level of competition. Having and using an athlete's mental strength is important because it can impact their ability to overcome challenges, handle pressure, and maintain focus.

By fostering mental toughness, coaches help athletes reach their full potential both during practice and competition.

Defining and Describing Mental Strength

Three components of mental strength are:

Self-Confidence: Believing in one's abilities and skills. Self-confidence helps athletes take risks and perform under pressure.

Resilience: The capacity to bounce back from setbacks and strive toward goals. Resilience helps athletes recover from mistakes and maintain motivation.

Focus: The ability to concentrate on the task and avoid distractions. Focus ensures that athletes can stay on track and execute their strategies effectively.

Why Is Understanding Mental Strength Important for Coaches?

It's not enough just to "know" what mental strength is; understanding mental strength is important for coaches as it allows them to better support their athletes' psychological needs. A coach who can recognize and adjust their style and approach to help athletes develop these traits will result in an adaptable athlete who will most likely excel over an athlete who does not have the same coping or support systems. The difference between a coach who knows and understands mental strength and an athlete who chooses to continue on amidst adversity can be the difference between someone who might give up and walk away.

A foundation in mental strength enables coaches to:

- Identify and address mental barriers that might affect performance.

- Implement strategies to build confidence, resilience, and focus.

- Provide better support during high-pressure situations, ensuring athletes remain calm and effective.

The Role of a Coach

A coach's role is multifaceted and requires a mix of professional and personal traits.

Professionally, a coach must be:

Knowledgeable: Understand the sport's technical aspects and training methods.

Communicative: Effectively convey instructions and feedback.

Motivational: Inspire and encourage athletes to reach their potential.

Analytical: Assess performance and make strategic decisions.

Adaptable: Adjust coaching methods to fit different athletes' needs and situations.

Personally, a coach should:

Passionate: Have a deep love for the sport and coaching, which naturally will result in enthusiasm and commitment.

Empathetic: Understand and relate to athletes' feelings and challenges, building trust and rapport.

Patient: Demonstrate patience and persistence, especially when working with athletes who face difficulties.

Different Techniques, Different Coaching Styles

Just as an athlete has different strengths and weaknesses, there are different coaching styles.

Each style can be beneficial for the right athlete; if not, it can do more harm than one may realize (Kim et al., 2021).

Authoritarian Coaching:

>**Pros**: Clear structure and expectations, effective in enforcing discipline.
>
>**Cons**: It may stifle creativity and autonomy, and can lead to resentment.
>
>**Best for**: Athletes who thrive on clear instructions and high discipline.

Democratic Coaching:

>**Pros**: Encourages athlete input and fosters a sense of ownership and collaboration.
>
>**Cons**: Decision-making can be slower and require more direction if managed well.

Best for: Athletes who are motivated by collaboration and team input.

Holistic Coaching:

Pros: Focuses on the athlete's overall well-being, including mental and emotional health.

Cons: It can be time-consuming and may require additional resources.

Best for: Athletes who need a balanced approach with psychological and physical support.

Transactional Coaching:

Pros: Provides clear rewards and consequences, which can motivate performance.

Cons: May not address deeper psychological issues or foster long-term development.

Best for: Athletes who respond well to structured incentives and accountability.

Transformational Coaching:

Pros: Inspires athletes to exceed their limits and achieve personal growth.

Cons: Requires a strong relationship and can be challenging to implement consistently.

Best for: Athletes seeking personal development and high levels of motivation.

Do's and Don'ts of Coaching

However, a few do's and don'ts can help with every coaching style. Here are a few to be mindful of (Murray et al., 2020):

Do's:

Communicate clearly and consistently.

Set realistic goals and expectations.

Provide constructive feedback.

Encourage effort and perseverance.

Foster a positive team environment.

Show respect and understanding.

Tailor coaching methods to individual needs.

Promote a healthy balance between competition and enjoyment.

Support athletes in managing stress and pressure.

Continue learning and adapting coaching strategies.

Don'ts:

Avoid negative criticism and humiliation.

Don't favor certain athletes over others.

Avoid being overly controlling or micromanaging.

Don't ignore an athlete's mental or emotional state.

Avoid inconsistency in rules and expectations.

Pay attention to the importance of recovery and rest.

Avoid setting unrealistic or unattainable goals.

Don't disregard athletes' feedback or concerns.

Avoid showing favoritism in decision-making.

Don't focus solely on winning at the expense of athlete development.

Impacts of Doing These "Don'ts":

- **Decreased Motivation**: Athletes may lose motivation if they feel unfairly treated or constantly criticized.

- **Increased Anxiety**: Ignoring mental and emotional needs can lead to increased stress and anxiety.

- **Diminished Performance**: Over-controlling or setting unrealistic goals can hinder an athlete's development and performance.

By understanding and implementing these principles, coaches can better support their athletes in developing physical and mental strength.

Parents as Pillars of Support

What do athletes like Tiger Woods, Serena and Venus Williams, Devin Booker, and Darren Ferguson have in common? They were coached by their parents (Barman, 2023).

Coaches don't have to be people who aren't family—in the cases of these well-known athletes, their parents played the role of coach and mentor.

The Role of the Parent to Athletes

Parents not only have the important role of providing love, care, and support, but they also play a crucial role in developing their budding young athlete when they choose to be coaches. Given their relationship to the athlete, this role can influence an athlete's journey directly and indirectly.

While a parent's support can be beneficial, it can also create challenges if there is no clear distinction or separation of the roles. For example, when both the athlete and coach are at home, do they discuss training or the matches? Or do they focus on the chores, homework, etc.? It is important to create boundaries; not doing so can negatively impact the relationship.

It is important that parents understand their various roles when they take on the role of coach and the potential impact of their involvement, as it can create a negative or positive environment (Baxter-Jones & Maffulli, 2003).

Direct and Indirect Implications of Parental Influence

Parents can impact their athlete children in several ways, both directly and indirectly:

Direct Influence Through Expectations:

Parents can directly impact their child's athletic experience by setting too high expectations. While high expectations can serve as motivation and drive athletes to strive for excellence, if the expectations are unrealistic or overly demanding, they can lead to pressure, anxiety, and even burnout for the athlete. If the lines between parent and coach are not established, they can also result in resentment.

Indirect Influence Through Behavior Modeling:

On the other hand, parents can indirectly influence their children by modeling positive behaviors. For example, how a parent handles success, failure, or stress can significantly affect how the young athlete approaches similar situations. A parent who demonstrates resilience and a positive attitude demonstrates to their athlete that they, too, can be mentally tough and persevere.

Emotional Support:

Parents acting as coaches also play an important role in emotional support. Athletes who feel supported and understood are more likely to have confidence in their abilities and feel secure in their endeavors. Young athletes may struggle with self-doubt and fear of failure without this support.

The Role of the Parent to Athletes

While the role of coach may be another title for a parent, there are other roles they may also play with their athlete. Here are other roles a parent/coach may take on.

Cheerleader:

Parents, as cheerleaders, provide the motivation and positive reinforcement that young athletes need to continue pursuing their sport. This role is important as it helps build self-esteem and reinforces the child's passion for the sport.

Mentor:

In the mentor role, parents provide guidance and advice based on their own personal experiences. This role is valuable in helping athletes navigate challenges, set realistic goals, and develop a strong work ethic.

Financial Supporter:

It is no secret that competitive sports can be expensive; as a result, parents often take on the role of financial supporter. This includes covering equipment, training, and travel costs, which are critical for providing young athletes with the necessary resources to succeed. As a financial supporter, parents must never use this to motivate or push their athletes to be better. For example, a parent/coach should never say, "If you don't win, I'll stop paying for training"—this can result in low self-esteem and worth.

Emotional Anchor:

Parents can act as emotional anchors, providing a safe space for athletes to express their frustrations and feelings. This emotional stability is crucial for helping young athletes cope with competitive pressures and maintain their mental well-being.

Role Model:

Parents serve as role models by demonstrating values such as discipline, hard work, and integrity. By embodying these traits, parents can instill similar values in their children, essential for success on and off the field.

Finding the Balance

Similarly, as athletes may struggle to balance their roles, parents can also struggle to balance their roles of parent and coach/supporter (Armstrong, 2023).

What can make finding the balance between coaching and parenting hard?

Here are a few reasons:

Unconscious Expectations:

Parents may have unconscious expectations for their child's athletic performance, often a result of past experiences or unfulfilled dreams. These expectations can create unnecessary pressure and result in unrealistic goals, which in turn cause stress for the child.

Deflecting Desires:

Sometimes, parents project their own unfulfilled desires onto their children, pushing them towards goals that they themselves may not have fulfilled when they were younger. Unfortunately, this can result in the child feeling obligated to meet these expectations, which may not align with their own aspirations. Or the athlete may feel they must be successful as they owe their parent.

Difficulty in Separating Roles:

It can be challenging for parents to separate their role as loving parents from that of coaches or supporters. This difficulty can lead to confusion and stress for the child, who may struggle to distinguish between parental guidance and coaching criticism; therefore, having open lines of communication as well as boundaries will help with this separation.

How to Give Support On and Off the Field

There are many ways to provide support; more importantly, the support given on and off the field will not always be the same (G, 2013).

Here are some tips on how a parent/coach can provide positive and constructive feedback and support.

On the Field:

Positive Reinforcement:

Positive reinforcement after successes and failures helps athletes build confidence and resilience.

Encouragement of Effort:

Regardless of the outcome, encouraging effort teaches athletes that trying their best is what truly matters.

Modelling Composure:

Parents who model composure during games teach their children to remain calm under pressure, a key component of mental toughness.

Cheering Respectfully:

Cheering in a way that supports the team and respects the game sets a positive example for young athletes.

Avoiding Over-Coaching:

Parents should avoid over-coaching from the sidelines, as this can undermine the coach's authority and confuse the athlete.

Off the Field:

Active Listening:

Listening to the athlete's concerns and feelings off the field shows that their emotions matter and provides emotional support.

Encouraging Balance:

Encouraging a balanced lifestyle, where sports are just one part of life, helps prevent burnout and promotes overall well-being.

Unconditional Support:

Offering unconditional support, regardless of performance, fosters a secure environment where athletes can thrive.

Fostering Independence:

Allowing athletes to make their own decisions and learn from their experiences helps build independence and confidence.

Parents play a multifaceted role in the lives of their athletic children. While their support can be invaluable, they must balance being a parent and a coach/supporter. By doing so, they can help their children develop the skills and mindset needed to succeed in sports and life.

A Winning Combination—the Parent Coach Duo

Having a parent as a coach can result in the ultimate and really winning combination of a support system for an athlete. They have a parent who provides unconditional love, motivation, and encouragement and a coach who shares their expertise, discipline, and strategic insights. However, it's important to remember that while it can be a winning combination, it is important to create those boundaries to prevent and mitigate any unwanted conflicts between athlete and coach or parent and child.

Along with creating boundaries, establishing and having open lines of communication and regular check-ins can help maintain the separation of roles.

Quiz Time

Coaches: What's Your Coaching Style?

1. When planning training sessions, you prioritize:

    a) Fun and engagement
    b) Skill development and technique
    c) Strategy and competition readiness

2. How do you handle a player who is struggling with performance?

    a) Offer encouragement and focus on their strengths
    b) Provide detailed feedback and extra practice
    c) Analyze their performance and adjust their role in the team

3. During a game, you are most likely to:

    a) Cheer on your players and keep the mood positive
    b) Give specific instructions and correct mistakes immediately
    c) Focus on game strategy and make tactical decisions

4. How do you develop your team's skills and abilities?

    a) Use fun drills and activities to keep players motivated
    b) Break down skills into fundamentals and build from there
    c) Implement complex drills that simulate game scenarios

5. When addressing team discipline, you:

    a) Emphasize respect and sportsmanship
    b) Set clear rules and consistently enforce them
    c) Focus on the consequences of actions and their impact on the team

6. Your approach to team building is to:

    a) Organize social activities and team bonding events
    b) Conduct regular team meetings and skill workshops
    c) Create a competitive environment to push players to work together

7. How do you handle conflicts within the team?

    a) Mediate and ensure everyone feels heard and valued
    b) Address issues directly and provide solutions
    c) Focus on how the resolution will benefit team performance

8. Your long-term goal for your team is:

    a) Ensure everyone enjoys playing and stays involved in the sport
    b) Develop well-rounded athletes with strong fundamentals
    c) Build a winning team that excels in competition

Analyzing Your Results:

Mostly A's: The Positive Motivator

You prioritize fun and motivation, ensuring players enjoy their experience and feel encouraged. Your coaching style fosters a positive environment where players feel supported and valued.

Mostly B's: The Technical Trainer

You focus on skill development and technique. Your coaching style emphasizes detailed instruction and consistent improvement, helping players to build a strong foundation in their sport.

Mostly C's: The Strategic Competitor

You prioritize strategy and competition readiness. Your coaching style is geared towards maximizing team performance and achieving competitive success, with a strong focus on tactics and game planning.

Parents: What's Your Communication Style?

1. When your child talks about their day, you:

    a) Listen attentively and ask open-ended questions
    b) Offer advice and solutions to any problems they mention
    c) Encourage them to reflect on their experiences and learn from them

2. How do you handle disagreements with your child?

    a) Stay calm and try to understand their perspective
    b) Explain your reasoning clearly and assertively
    c) Look for a compromise that satisfies both of you

3. When your child is upset, you typically:

    a) Offer comfort and let them express their feelings
    b) Help them identify the problem and find a solution
    c) Encourage them to think about what they can learn from the situation

4. How do you praise your child?

    a) Frequently and for any effort or accomplishment
    b) Specifically, and based on their achievements and improvements
    c) Focus on their personal growth and development over time

5. When setting rules or expectations, you:

    a) Discuss them with your child and get their input
    b) Clearly state the rules and the consequences of breaking them
    c) Explain the reasoning behind the rules and the benefits of following them

6. Your approach to helping your child with challenges is to:

    a) Support them emotionally and boost their confidence
    b) Provide guidance and practical solutions
    c) Encourage them to problem-solve and think critically

7. How do you celebrate your child's successes?

    a) With lots of praise and positive reinforcement
    b) By acknowledging their hard work and dedication
    c) By highlighting what they learned and how they grew

8. When your child makes a mistake, you:

    a) Reassure them that everyone makes mistakes
    b) Discuss what went wrong and how to fix it
    c) Encourage them to reflect on the mistake and what they can do differently next time

Analyzing Your Results:

Mostly A's: The Empathetic Listener

You prioritize emotional support and understanding. Your communication style fosters a trusting and open relationship, making your child feel valued and heard.

Mostly B's: The Practical Problem-Solver

You focus on providing advice and solutions. Your communication style is geared towards helping your child overcome obstacles and improve their practical skills.

Mostly C's: The Reflective Guide

You emphasize learning and personal growth. Your communication style encourages your child to think critically about their experiences and develop a deeper understanding of themselves and their world.

Chapter 3:

Dream Big—
Goal Setting and Motivation

There's no way around hard work. Embrace it. You have to put in the hours because there is always something you can improve on. –Roger Federer

From Vision to Reality—Setting Goals

Budding athletes around the world dream of one day winning the Stanley Cup, making it to the World Cup, or playing in the Olympics. While these dreams may seem out of reach for some, they become attainable for those who are determined to make them a reality. What does it take to make it to the Olympic podium or to raise that Stanley Cup high and proud? It is a result of intense training, planning, and goal-setting. The journey of imagining these dreams into reality and actually achieving them is where the magic of goal-setting comes into play.

Superstar athletes Sydney Crosby, Lionel Messi, and Simone Biles didn't just dream of greatness—they planned for it. Winning the Stanley Cup, participating in the World Cup, and competing in the Olympics are monumental achievements that require a lifetime of dedication and, sometimes, sacrifice.

What do these athletes have in common, aside from winning gold, the Stanley Cup, and the World Cup? Their dreams were all achievable with a clear and actionable plan.

Goals are stepping stones that bridge the gap between one's vision and reality while providing a structured approach to achieving these dreams.

Why Set Goals?

Individuals and athletes set specific, measurable, and time-bound targets to achieve their goals. Unlike our sometimes out-of-this-world goals, which can sometimes feel overwhelming, setting goals with tangible milestones helps break down that larger vision into manageable tasks. As one expert puts it, "Goals provide clarity and direction, making the path to success not only visible but attainable" (Weinberg, 2013).

In the context of athletes and sports, goals serve several purposes. First, they help an athlete maintain focus. For example, an athlete aiming to compete in the Olympics might set a goal to improve their performance in specific areas, such as increasing their endurance over the next six months. Another thing goals do is provide motivation. Knowing that each training session brings them one step closer to that critical match can help keep them focused and committed to their training. Thirdly, goals offer a way to measure progress, helping athletes adjust their strategies as needed to stay on track (Weinberg & Gould, 2010).

To be successful and attainable, goals must be specific, measurable, and achievable, providing a clear roadmap to success.

How to Set Goals

Goal-setting isn't just about writing down what you want to achieve and then doing it. If it were this easy, everyone would achieve their goals, and this book would not be needed. The reality is that not everyone knows how to set goals or how to achieve them. Setting goals is about following a structured approach that will increase the likelihood of you getting to the end.

A popular method for setting goals is the SMART approach, which stands for Specific, Measurable, Achievable, Relevant, and Time-bound.

Following this formula ensures that goals are clear and attainable, which is crucial for maintaining motivation and focus (Locke & Latham, 1990).

When athletes fail to set realistic goals, or they think they can skip steps to get to the end, this is usually indicative that their goals are either unrealistic or unattainable the way they are doing them. This can result in frustration and a lack of motivation.

For example, an athlete who sets a goal to run a marathon in under three hours within a month, despite never having run more than a few miles at a time, is setting themselves up for failure. If they had been training for months, then this would be a more realistic and attainable goal rather than just thinking they can run and achieve it.

SMART Goals

Using the SMART technique is a powerful tool for athletes who want to turn their visions into reality.

Each component of SMART goals plays a critical role in the goal-setting process:

Specific: Goals should be clear and unambiguous. For example, instead of saying, "I want to get better at soccer," a more specific goal would be, "I want to improve my dribbling skills to successfully maneuver past opponents during games."

Measurable: Athletes need to track their progress. A measurable goal might be, "I aim to complete 10 successful dribbles in each game this season."

Achievable: Goals should be challenging yet attainable. An achievable goal could be, "I will practice dribbling for 30 minutes daily to enhance my skills."

Relevant: Goals must align with the athlete's broader objectives. If the athlete dreams of becoming a top scorer, improving dribbling skills is directly applicable.

Time-bound: Setting a deadline creates urgency and focus. A time-bound goal could be, "I aim to improve my dribbling skills within three months."

By setting SMART goals, athletes can ensure that their efforts are focused and productive, bringing them closer to their dreams one step at a time (Doran, 1981).

Linking Values and Our Athletic Goals

While it's not often discussed or thought of as having any links to sports and goals, an athlete's values are core elements that guide their behavior and decisions. In athletics, they play a crucial role in shaping the goals an athlete sets out to achieve and how they plan to work on achieving them. Values like discipline, perseverance, and integrity often underpin the goals that athletes set for themselves, ensuring that their ambitions align with their core beliefs (Jones et al., 2002).

For instance, an athlete who values discipline might set a goal to never miss a training session, while an athlete who values teamwork might set a goal to improve communication with teammates. These values help ensure that the goals are not just about achieving success but, more importantly, align with what the athlete believes and stands by.

Knowing Your Values

Athletes, especially competitive ones, must be able to identify their values before setting goals. Doing this will help ensure that the goals they set are not only achievable but meaningful as well. When athletes set goals that align with their values, they are more likely to stay committed and motivated, even when faced with challenges (Jones et al., 2002).

Conversely, when athletes pursue goals that don't align with their values, they may feel unmotivated and discouraged. For example, an athlete who values sportsmanship may feel hollow after winning a game through unsportsmanlike conduct. This disconnect between values and goals can result in dissatisfaction and lack of motivation.

Fueling Our Fire

As mentioned, the road to achieving and accomplishing goals is rarely smooth and without obstacles. Therefore, it is perfectly natural that athletes encounter setbacks and challenges that can test their determination. These challenges can be discouraging, whether it's dealing with an injury, facing a losing streak, or struggling to move forward in your division. It's important to remember that setbacks are a natural part of the journey, and overcoming them is what will fuel our growth and development as athletes.

When we experience setbacks such as not making the team, losing a critical game, or failing to meet a personal best, how we move forward and grow from these is the real test. In these moments, finding motivation and inspiration is important. That motivation might come from within or from external sources, like the support of a coach or family member.

For some athletes, it may not always be easy to see this perspective but it's important to recognize that setbacks are not failures, but rather opportunities to learn, adapt, and come back stronger (Jones et al., 2002).

Finding Motivation Amongst Frustration

When we find ourselves faced with a problem or obstacle, what will dictate whether we move forward or backward is our motivation. Motivation is a key driving force that helps athletes push through their frustrations and continue working toward their goals.

There are several ways athletes can find and harness motivation:

Revisiting their goals: Reminding themselves of their goals and why they set them can reignite their passion.

Seeking inspiration from others: Whether watching a documentary about a favorite athlete or reading about someone who overcame similar challenges, finding role models can be a powerful motivator.

Breaking down goals into smaller tasks: Tackling smaller, more manageable tasks can help athletes build momentum and regain motivation.

Focusing on progress: Celebrating small wins and recognizing progress can boost morale and motivate athletes.

Leaning on support networks: Family, friends, and coaches can provide the encouragement and support needed to keep going.

Why Do We Lose Motivation?

Imagine finding that after all those long hours of training, you still come in second place; this can be frustrating, which can result in losing motivation to continue. Other common reasons for losing motivation include burnout, lack of progress or wanted results, and external pressures. When athletes lose motivation, this can impact their mental and emotional well-being, leading to feelings of inadequacy and self-doubt.

For example, an athlete whose peers consistently outperform them might begin to doubt their abilities and lose motivation to continue training. This lack of motivation can hinder their performance and affect their relationships with teammates and coaches, creating a negative feedback loop that's hard to break.

Common Obstacles Athletes Face

Often, athletes face numerous obstacles on their journey to greatness. Some of the most common include:

Injuries: Physical injuries can sideline athletes, disrupting their training and impacting their confidence.

> **Tip**: Focus on rehabilitation and use the downtime to work on mental skills, such as visualization.

Performance anxiety: The pressure to perform can lead to anxiety, which can negatively impact performance.

> **Tip**: To manage anxiety, practice relaxation techniques, such as deep breathing.

Burnout: Overtraining can lead to burnout, resulting in fatigue and a lack of motivation.

> **Tip**: Ensure a balanced training schedule that includes rest and recovery.

External pressures: Expectations from coaches, parents, or the athletes themselves can create stress and anxiety.

> **Tip**: Set realistic goals and communicate openly with support networks.

Self-doubt: Athletes may struggle with self-doubt, especially after a poor performance.

> **Tip**: Focus on past successes and use positive self-talk to boost confidence.

Overcoming these obstacles is not just about physical toughness but mental toughness as well. Acknowledging and addressing the challenges that may be preventing progress and then developing the necessary strategies to overcome them means that one can continue to make progress toward one's why one may not be progressing goals (Jones et al., 2002).

Intrinsic vs. Extrinsic Motivation

Understanding why we lose motivation is just as important as understanding what motivates us. Motivation can be classified into two categories: intrinsic and extrinsic.

Intrinsic motivation is fueled by personal satisfaction and passion for the activity, while extrinsic motivation is driven by external factors such as rewards, acknowledgment, or influence from others (Ryan & Deci, 2000).

Knowing the Difference

Athletes and coaches should know and understand the difference between intrinsic and extrinsic motivation, as understanding their motivations can help them direct and position their goals to be achievable.

Intrinsic motivation is much easier to maintain and often leads to greater satisfaction and long-term commitment to the sport. Conversely, while effective from a short-term perspective, extrinsic motivation can lead to burnout if it becomes the sole driving force behind an athlete's efforts. For instance, an athlete who is solely motivated by the desire to win may lose interest in the sport if they do not achieve the desired outcome.

The one thing that rings true though is that an athlete who is motivated by a genuine love for the game is more likely to remain committed, even in the face of setbacks.

Staying Motivated and Positive

Staying motivated isn't always about being happy or positive. It's about maintaining a sense of purpose while finding ways to stay motivated and move forward, even when you may want to give up. Using this notion of positive psychology, which focuses on building strengths rather than fixing weaknesses, can play a significant role in helping athletes stay motivated.

It encourages athletes to focus and use their strengths, which leads to a growth mindset. A growth mindset means that the athlete is focused on what they can control and celebrates victories, no matter how small or big.

Template—Goal Setting

Use the SMART acronym and define your goal. Create short, medium and long-term goals.

Consider the following prompts when goal-setting:

- What are the specific steps I need to take to achieve my goal?

- How can I measure my progress towards my athletic goals?

- What potential obstacles could prevent me from reaching my goals, and how can I overcome them?

- What is my timeline for achieving my athletic goals, and is it realistic?

- Are my goals challenging enough to motivate me but also attainable with hard work and dedication?

- Have I set short-term and long-term athletic goals to keep me focused and motivated?

- Am I willing to make the necessary sacrifices and adjustments in my lifestyle to achieve my athletic goals?

- Have I sought input from my coaches, trainers, or teammates to help refine and clarify my athletic goals?

- How will achieving these goals positively impact my performance and overall athletic career?

- What strategies and tactics must I employ to maintain my motivation and momentum toward my athletic goals?

Quiz Time: What's Your Motivation?

1. When you think about your training sessions, you are most excited by:

   a) Improving your personal performance
   b) Winning competitions and gaining recognition
   c) Being part of a team and contributing to its success
   d) The physical and mental benefits of exercise

2. How do you feel when you achieve a personal best or a new milestone?

   a) Proud and accomplished
   b) Motivated to achieve even more
   c) Happy to share the success with teammates and coaches
   d) Satisfied with the progress and the effort

3. What drives you to keep practicing even when it's tough?

   a) The desire to constantly improve and reach new goals
   b) The ambition to be the best and win awards
   c) The support and encouragement from your team
   d) The enjoyment of the activity and its health benefits

4. When setting goals, you usually focus on:

   a) Personal performance targets and skill development
   b) Achieving specific awards or rankings
   c) Team achievements and group goals
   d) Maintaining a healthy and balanced lifestyle

5. During a game or competition, what keeps you pushing forward?

   a) The challenge of pushing your limits
   b) The thought of winning and being recognized
   c) The camaraderie and support of your teammates
   d) The fun and enjoyment of playing the sport

6. How do you react to setbacks or failures?

   a) Analyze what went wrong and work on improving
   b) Use them as fuel to come back stronger and win next time
   c) Rely on your team for support and encouragement
   d) Accept them as part of the journey and focus on the positives

7. What aspect of being an athlete do you find most rewarding?

   a) Personal growth and skill improvement
   b) Success and recognition in competitions
   c) Building relationships and teamwork
   d) The overall health and wellness benefits

8. How do you prefer to celebrate your achievements?

   a) Setting new goals and challenges
   b) Enjoying the spotlight and recognition
   c) Celebrating with your team and supporters
   d) Reflecting on the journey and the hard work

Analyzing Your Results

Mostly A's: Personal Growth and Mastery

You are motivated by the desire to improve and master your skills. Your personal achievements and continuous progress drive you.

Mostly B's: Recognition and Success

You are driven by the ambition to win and gain recognition. Achievements, awards, and being the best are your primary motivators.

Mostly C's: Teamwork and Camaraderie

You thrive on the support and connection with your team. Being part of a group and contributing to collective success is what keeps you motivated.

Mostly D's: Health and Enjoyment

You are motivated by the activity's enjoyment and its health benefits. Your main focus is the overall experience and well-being.

Chapter 4:

The Key to Success: Confidence

Belief in oneself is incredibly infectious. It generates momentum, the collective force of which far outweighs any kernel of self-doubt that may creep in. –Aimee Mullins

Building the Foundation?

Imagine standing in front of a crowd of hundreds, if not thousands, of people cheering your name. Amongst the crowd are people who are probably also booing you too—but despite those negative jeers, you do your routine, you take your shot, and you score, or maybe you miss. Whatever it is, you did what so many are too afraid to do—why? Confidence.

When it comes to mental toughness, confidence is a stepping stone that, like the situation above, can be important in how one reacts to pressure. Confidence drives an athlete to stand tall and proud, trust in their skills, and know they can achieve what they need, regardless of the outcome (Trine University, 2023).

Confidence also plays an important role for athletes who compete competitively. It is the foundation on which athletes rely when it comes to dealing with pressures they may not be necessarily accustomed to. Performing in front of a crowd, racing the final lap, or whatever the situation, confidence can boost athletes to know they can do it.

Where Does My Confidence Come From?

If confidence is the key to an athlete's journey to mental toughness, where does it come from? Confidence is one of those innate traits that can be developed but also nurtured through practice, experience, and positive encouragement. The combination of past successes and experiences results in a strong sense of self-belief and confidence (Trine University, 2023).

For some, confidence is natural; it is a result of their upbringing and environment, while for others, it is, as mentioned, learned. Those who go the route of learning to be confident get it by overcoming and dealing with the barriers and challenges, therefore resulting in a boost of confidence.

Confidence Boosters and Techniques

While being born with a natural aura of confidence is great for some, for many, developing this trait and persona takes practice, patience, and a shift in mindset.

Here are a few ways one can boost their confidence:

Positive Self-Talk: Encouraging oneself with affirmations and positive statements can help reinforce confidence and minimize self-doubt.

Visualization: Visualizing your success and mentally rehearsing what you will do to accomplish and achieve your goals can help you mentally prepare and boost your confidence and self-assurance.

Setting Achievable Goals: Breaking down those large, lofty goals into smaller, much more manageable ones. With each small milestone achieved, this will help the athlete see their progress and, in turn, boost their confidence.

Focus on Your Strength, Not Weakness: Concentrating on what you do well versus what you don't will boost your confidence, and slowly, you will find yourself wanting to improve those areas that aren't as strong.

Practice, Practice, Practice: Confidence comes from knowing you are prepared (mentally, physically, and emotionally); therefore, consistency and practice are essential for boosting confidence.

While these techniques scratch the surface of boosting one's self-confidence, here are some empowering mantras to help when feeling doubt and insecurity.

- I am capable of achieving my goals
- I have trust in my training, and I am prepared
- Every setback is an opportunity to grow and come back better
- I am strong, resilient, and unstoppable
- Success is the result of hard work and persistence
- Nothing in life comes easy
- Success is the reward of all my hard work and training

These are just a few examples of mantras that serve as reminders of an athlete's potential and can be quite powerful in countering the sometimes easier to fall into the mentality of negativity (Cohn, 2018).

Hitting Back at Self-Doubt

Athlete or not, self-doubt is a common challenge faced by many. This feeling is often heightened when you face stress or a setback, and it can result in a lack of motivation, hesitation or poor performance and decision-making. When athletes struggle or can't embrace their accomplishments, this is often a result of a deep-seated belief that they are not deserving or worthy. They often will not see their accomplishments as their own but rather due to others—for example, an athlete with high self-doubt may think the only reason they won a tournament is that their opponent had an off day or that their coach did something (Trine University, 2023). This self-doubt negates their own hard work, training and efforts.

Sometimes, this feeling of incompetence can be exacerbated by negative self-worth, coaches, or parents and their pressure and expectations.

Why Do We Struggle to Embrace Success?

If you have never won or known success, it can be almost foreign and intimidating when you finally get a taste of it. In some cases, athletes fear success, as it means there may be more pressure to maintain that level of success.

Two reasons athletes struggle with embracing and accepting their success and victories are:

1. **Increased expectation**: After a win, an athlete may feel as though they have to perform to win continually, and if they don't, they won't have the support, encouragement, or love of their friends and family.

2. **Imposter Syndrome**: This idea of imposter syndrome is fairly common among athletes and people who feel they don't deserve their success. Athletes who experience this feeling tend to experience high levels of stress and anxiety but try to mask it from others.

While it would make sense that athletes should revel in their wins and accomplishments, this is much easier said than done. Therefore, it is important for the athlete and the coach and support system to remind them they worked for what they received. This type of support and words of encouragement can help the athlete shift their negative narrative and insecurities towards confidence and assurance.

Not All Failures Are Bad

Along with struggling to embrace and celebrate their successes, athletes also tend to view failures as negative; however, not all failures are bad.

Failing is actually a natural part of an athlete's journey; it is one filled with lessons learned and opportunities for growth. Just because an athlete did not receive a medal or win that final playoff doesn't mean they should give up—rather, they can use this opportunity to improve and refine their skills and strategies, but more importantly, build resilience.

Consider an athlete who gets injured during a playoff match. Rather than sulk and see this as a lost moment, they should perceive it as an opportunity to stop, take a moment, and appreciate the journey to recovering and getting better for their next match. It is common amongst athletes who get injured to want to instantly get back to playing; however, being injured can remind them that they need to be patient and see this as a growing moment.

Another example of a failure that isn't as bad is a team that loses the playoffs. They could simply take their loss, blame the referees, one another, or they can come together and work towards improving for the next match.

Moments like these are a good reminder that failure is not the opposite of success; it's part of the journey of developing and mastering one's skills. Embracing our failures is an opportunity to learn, be humble, and grow.

Strategies to Overcome Self-Doubt

Between trying to embrace and celebrate our victories and dealing with self-doubt, here are six tips on overcoming doubt.

Where does this doubt stem from? It is often a result of fear—fear of the unknown and fear of judgment, and as athletes, fear can sometimes push one to give up on one's dreams and potential.

So, the next time you experience self-doubt, try some of the following:

Acknowledge the Doubt: The moment an inkling of doubt arises, don't fuel it. Confront it and recognize that "you" are doubting yourself (Trine University, 2023)

Redirect and Reframe Negativity: Replace negative thoughts with positive ones. For example, instead of saying, "I can't do this," flip the situation around and say, "I will do my best, learn, and enjoy this moment."

Celebrate Your Victories: Celebrate all your achievements, no matter how big or small. Doing this will build your confidence and motivation to move forward.

Ask for Help: It's okay to get help; it's even more okay to ask for it. When you experience moments of self-doubt, reach out to your coach and mentor and discuss your feelings. They can provide you with the assurance you need, but more importantly, they will be honest.

Be Mindful: Assess and know when you find yourself being triggered or feeling doubt, and take a pause. Remind yourself that you have been training, that you know yourself, but more importantly, recognize the signs of doubt creeping in.

Goal Setting: Remember how we talked about the importance of goals? Setting goals, especially smaller milestones, will help you overcome those moments of self-doubt. It will also allow you to get a pulse on your progress.

Fueled by Naysayers

While we wish everyone would love us, the reality is that there will always be the naysayers. The ones who try to tear you down—despite you being a great athlete or being confident, they will always find a way to make you doubt or belittle your accomplishments.

Remember that what these naysayers say doesn't have to be negative; it doesn't have to hold you back or make you question yourself. With the right mindset, you can use the criticism and noise as feedback to improve.

Sometimes, the best revenge is proving those who thought it not possible wrong (Trine University, 2023)!

Handling Criticism—the Good and the Bad

Typically, naysayers will offer their two-cents and mask it as feedback. While this may or may not be true, criticism can be both constructive and destructive.

Constructive criticism, even from a naysayer, can provide feedback on some aspect of your performance that you may not be aware needs improving. Typically, constructive criticism is about an action or behavior rather than personal.

On the other hand, destructive criticism, which typically is what naysayers do, is vague, personal, and often meant to undermine an athlete's confidence. If you aren't mentally prepared or you haven't trained yourself, this undermining can lead to self-doubt and feelings of inadequacy. Destructive criticism is more about tearing down than building up the athlete.

Learning to distinguish between the types of criticism is key, and it will help you, as an athlete, when you hear the noise from naysayers.

Remember, at the end of the day, you have control of your thoughts—reframe the negative or, better yet, ignore those naysayers and focus on yourself.

Staying Optimistic and Resilient

The moment you allow the naysayers and negativity to hold you back, you are letting all the factors you can't control win. It's important to remember your strengths and that you are the one who is on the court, not them. By remaining resilient and optimistic, you are overcoming one of the biggest challenges athletes face—criticism and negativity.

Stay focused on your goals and use the feedback, regardless of who it's coming from and build on your success and growth. You know yourself better than anybody—don't let anyone tell you otherwise.

Quiz Time: How's Your Confidence?

1. When preparing for a competition, you typically feel:

    a) Nervous and unsure about your performance
    b) Somewhat anxious but generally optimistic
    c) Excited and confident about your abilities

2. How do you react to constructive criticism from coaches or teammates?

    a) Take it personally and feel discouraged
    b) Consider the feedback and try to apply it
    c) Welcome the feedback as a way to improve

3. In high-pressure situations, you tend to:

    a) Feel overwhelmed and doubt your abilities
    b) Stay focused but have some doubts
    c) Remain calm and trust your preparation

4. When you make a mistake during practice or competition, you:

    a) Dwell on it and lose confidence
    b) Feel disappointed but move on
    c) Learn from it and quickly refocus

5. How do you feel about your overall skills and abilities?

    a) Often doubt if you're good enough
    b) Recognize your strengths but also your weaknesses
    c) Believe in your skills and constantly strive to improve

6. Before a big game or event, you:

    a) Worry about how you'll perform
    b) Feel a mix of nerves and excitement
    c) Feel prepared and eager to compete

7. How do you handle unexpected changes or setbacks?

    a) Get easily frustrated and lose confidence
    b) Adapt but with some hesitation
    c) Stay flexible and confident in finding a solution

8. When you think about your future in your sport, you:

    a) Worry about whether you'll be successful
    b) Have some doubts but mostly positive expectations
    c) Feel confident and motivated to achieve your goals

Analyzing Your Results

Mostly A's: Building Confidence

You might struggle with self-doubt and low confidence. Focusing on positive self-talk, setting small, achievable goals, and celebrating your progress can help build your confidence.

Mostly B's: Moderate Confidence

You have a moderate level of confidence. Maintaining a positive mindset, seeking constructive feedback, and visualizing success can help strengthen your confidence.

Mostly C's: High Confidence

You demonstrate a high level of confidence. Continue to leverage your positive mindset, preparation, and resilience to maintain and build on your confidence.

Chapter 5:

The Power of Focus and Concentration

Losing is not my enemy; fear of losing is my enemy. –Rafael Nadal

When it comes to sports, having focus almost seems inevitable, but when you aren't mentally prepared or don't have the tools and support, focus can seem almost impossible. The best way to describe focus is the mental energy and concentration directed at a task. It means silencing outside distractions and having a heightened sense of awareness—as an athlete, this means being fully present and attentive.

Conversely, when athletes lack focus or attention, they begin to experience self-doubt and anxiety, and their chances of making mistakes increase. In the world of competitive sports, having a laser-sharp focus is crucial to performing at peak levels. This isn't to say that athletes who play recreational sports or are starting out don't need focus. Instead, focus is learned and finessed over time, and for recreational or beginner athletes, understanding their weaknesses and strengths will only further help them understand how much or little focus they have.

Finding Your Focus

While for some, knowing what they need to improve or focus on may be second nature, the truth is that it will vary from athlete to athlete. More importantly, athletes may not attribute their successes or lack thereof to a lack of focus or attention to detail. Remember, failing or mistakes aren't bad—they are stepping stones to improving; therefore, the same principle of focus is applied.

Learning and embracing where they may lack focus will help center an athlete on what they need to draw attention to.

How Does Focus and Concentration Impact Gameplay?

Although focus and concentration may be perceived as the same, they are distinct and intertwined. Both are almost necessary, especially for athletes, because concentration is the mental effort needed to focus. Without the other, athletes may find themselves having shortfalls on and off the field, such as a lack of patience, discipline, and attention; however, if athletes concentrate, they can focus on the task at hand.

Think of concentration as the glue that keeps focus in place; without concentration, our focus wavers. Athletes who engage in mental exercises such as visualization use concentration and focus. How? They concentrate on seeing their gameplay or routines, and by not giving in to distractions or getting sidetracked, they are focused. On the other hand, if the athlete practices visualization but then is invited to go out for pizza or to play video games, and they do, they are not focused; therefore, they are only practicing half the equation.

Mindfulness in Sports

We have heard of mindfulness—often associated with yoga or calming strategies—but it can also be used for competitive play. Since mindfulness is about maintaining a moment-by-moment awareness of our thoughts, feelings, and surroundings, when we lack focus or concentration, we also lack mindfulness.

Mindfulness in competitive sports means staying "in the zone" or focused. A mindful athlete can remain calm under pressure, make decisions under pressure, and be less likely to be impacted or affected by their competitors or taunts from outside factors (Brenner, 2023).

What about an athlete who isn't mindful? All the distractions a mindful athlete can easily ignore can affect them. The athlete who lacks mindfulness may act emotionally aggressive, which not only impacts their play but can also impact others. Their negativity and frustration don't just affect them; they can indirectly impact others; therefore, mental strength and mindfulness can help shut down these distractions.

Five ways to practice mindfulness include:

Breath Awareness: Focusing on breathing patterns helps calm the mind and body.

Visualization: Mental rehearsal of successful performances boosts confidence and focus.

Body Scan: Paying attention to bodily sensations to release tension and improve relaxation.

Mindful Movement: Practicing slow, deliberate movements to enhance physical awareness.

Gratitude Journaling: Reflecting on positive aspects of one's athletic journey to foster a positive mindset.

Even though the athlete may be completing the task, mindfulness benefits both the coach and the parents. It's a technique that can positively impact the overall environment, and a positive environment can affect a player's mindset (Straw, 2023).

Blocking Out Distractions

Distractions are part of the game, but how athletes manage them will make a difference between winning and losing, figuratively or literally. The top distractions that athletes face:

External Noises: Crowd reactions, competitors or environment

Internal Thoughts: Self-doubt, anxiety, stress, personal worries

Physical: Injury or discomfort

While these distractions are common, there are a few things that an athlete can do to counter them. To prevent distractions, athletes can have a pre-game ritual, engage in positive self-talk, or do what they can by minimizing distractions (*Dealing With Distraction*, 2021).

What does a pre-game ritual look like? It could be something as simple as having a special meal or turning off all phones or distractions before the match. Pre-games are rituals or traditions that athletes follow to help them get in the right mindset.

Why Do We Make Excuses?

The reality is we are all human, and sometimes, we just don't want to train or do the pre-game preparation we know will help us at game time. One of the reasons we make excuses is that we fear the possibility of failing or we know that we may not be as prepared or confident as we think. This negative attitude and lack of assurance can distract us and can be an easy scapegoat for not being fully trained or equipped.

Can we prevent or stop ourselves from making excuses? Yes, yes, you can!

Managing Distractions and Excuses

It all comes down to shifting our mindset. The moment we find ourselves being tested or distracted, athletes need to accept that this is part of the game, and sometimes, some distractions will be greater than others. As an athlete, if you shift your mindset and mentally prepare, then the distractions are just noise. Techniques such as mindfulness, goal-setting, and positive self-talk can help maintain focus and push through distractions and excuses.

A resilient mindset enables athletes to adapt to any challenges or pressures.

Identifying Distractions

Just as an athlete is guaranteed to play against competitors, being proactive and identifying distractions beforehand can mitigate them.

Identifying the distractions is the first step in managing them, but how can an athlete manage or identify them?

Asking questions such as:

- What is my main focus right now?

- Is this thought a positive or negative thought?

- I am feeling triggered or not focused; what can I do or say?

These few statements can help athletes identify what may distract them and mitigate or prevent it from affecting them.

Mentally Preparing and Training Our Mind

Having the mental preparation to cope and deal with distractions and pressures will help prepare the athlete, but more importantly, it will separate them from the winners and the losers. Shifting one's mindset to a positive one or recognizing those negative thoughts will train the athlete's mind and continue to build on resilience.

Training to compete is not just about training the body but also about training mentally and emotionally. Competitive athletes know the psychological demands and recognize the importance of preparing for the big game and the lead-up, which is just as important as the present moment.

Coping With Pressures

Athletes face internal and external pressures. Some are pressures they exert themselves, while others are exerted (directly or indirectly) by coaches, friends, and family. There are two types of pressures that athletes can face: internal and external. Internal pressures are ones that athletes put on themselves as a result of self-imposed expectations and goals. Internal pressures can sometimes lead to performance anxiety, self-doubt, and stress.

External pressures come from coaches, parents, or other outside factors. These pressures tend to accompany the expectation of performing to maintain an image or reputation.

Techniques to Cope With Pressure

How can athletes cope with the pressure of training or competing? Here are tips and techniques to cope with the pressure of performing:

Breathing Exercises: Helps calm the nervous system.

Visualization: Prepares the mind for success.

Positive Self-Talk: Reinforces confidence and reduces anxiety.

Goal Setting: Provides a clear focus and direction.

Progressive Muscle Relaxation: Reduces physical tension.

Routine Building: Establishes a sense of control and familiarity.

Journaling: Helps process emotions and thoughts.

Physical Exercise: Releases endorphins and reduces stress.

Mindfulness Meditation: Enhances focus and awareness.

Support Seeking: Reaching out for guidance and encouragement.

Distractions and pressures are just a few of the things that are part of being an athlete—but at the end of the day, what will matter the most is how one deals with them. If athletes can train their minds just as well as their bodies, they will be in good shape to handle any curve balls on and off the field.

Quiz Time: Am I Easily Distracted?

1. During practice, you find yourself:

    a) Frequently losing focus and thinking about other things
    b) Occasionally distracted but generally focused
    c) Fully immersed and attentive to the practice

2. When your coach is giving instructions, you:

    a) Often zone out and miss key points
    b) Listen but sometimes get distracted
    c) Pay close attention and remember details

3. During a game or competition, you:

    a) Easily get distracted by the crowd or other external factors
    b) Occasionally notice distractions but can refocus quickly
    c) Remain completely focused on the game

4. When performing repetitive drills, you:

    a) Get bored, and your mind wanders
    b) Stay focused most of the time but sometimes get distracted
    c) Stay fully engaged and concentrate on improving

5. How do you handle unexpected interruptions during practice or games?

    a) Get frustrated and lose focus
    b) Feel momentarily distracted but quickly regain focus
    c) Stay calm and refocus without much effort

6. When you set goals for a practice session, you:

    a) Often forget about them or get sidetracked
    b) Remember them but sometimes get distracted
    c) Stay committed and focused on achieving them

7. How do you manage distractions from your personal life during training?

    a) They frequently interfere with your focus
    b) They sometimes distract you, but you try to compartmentalize
    c) You effectively separate personal issues from training time

8. After making a mistake in practice or a game, you:

    a) Dwell on it and get distracted from the current task
    b) Feel distracted initially but then refocus
    c) Quickly move on and concentrate on the next play

Analyzing Your Results

Mostly A's: Easily Distracted

You might find it challenging to stay focused and easily get distracted. Working on mindfulness, setting clear goals, and developing a pre-performance routine can help improve your concentration.

Mostly B's: Moderately Distracted

You experience some distractions but can generally refocus. Enhancing your focus through mental training techniques and reducing potential distractions can help you stay more consistently focused.

Mostly C's: Highly Focused

You are skilled at maintaining focus and handling distractions. To stay at the top of your game, continue to use and refine your focus strategies.

Chapter 6:

Mastering Stress and Pressure

I can only control my performance. If I do my best, then I can feel good at the end of the day. –Michael Phelps

Imagine this...

High school basketball star Jamie is about to take the final shot in a playoff game. The gym is filled with loud cheers, coaches and players yelling, and amongst all this, Jamie feels the weight of the team and the coach's dreams of winning. Jamie starts to feel her heart racing, her hands sweat excessively, and her mind fills with doubt. Her mind goes blank. It is at this moment Jamie starts to experience performance anxiety—a common and sometimes misunderstood reality for competitive athletes.

Performance anxiety is not only common but sometimes misunderstood. The anxiety experienced doesn't only happen during a big game; it can happen during training or just out of the blue. Common signs of performance anxiety are increased heart rate, shaking hands, sweating and self-doubt (O'Rourke et al., 2011). All, if not most, athletes experience some form of performance anxiety; what distinguishes them from other athletes is their coping mechanisms.

Let's look back at the example at the beginning of the chapter and Jamie. She may be experiencing performance anxiety, but if Jamie has the proper tools, she can take a deep breath, close her eyes, and shift the negative self-talk to statements of "I got this" or "I've been training, and I'm ready." If Jamie's coach or teammates notice that she's experiencing performance anxiety, they can provide words of support or encouragement (Siegfried, 2024).

Stresses Athletes Face

Along with performance anxiety, athletes face performance pressure and stress, sometimes perceived and sometimes not. The pressures can be self-imposed or result from coaches, parents, or teammates. These pressures can be immense and can sometimes either make or break an athlete.

Coaches and parents can also contribute to stress, sometimes by making it a stressor without knowing it. These types of stressors, the unspoken or misguided ones, can impact an athlete's mentality and make them question their skillset.

Recognizing the Signs of Stress

Signs of stress aren't always apparent; sometimes, athletes will dismiss them as part of the game or think they are natural.

Some signs of stress include:

Physical Symptoms: Headaches, fatigue, insomnia, and changes in appetite.

Emotional Symptoms: Irritability, anxiety, depression, and mood swings.

Cognitive Symptoms: Difficulty concentrating, negative self-talk, and constant worry.

Behavioral Symptoms: Withdrawal from activities, increased use of alcohol or drugs, and changes in training habits.

Performance Issues: Decline in performance, mistakes during competitions, and loss of motivation.

In addition to being able to recognize the signs of stress, athletes experience unique stressors that most individuals don't get to experience.

Examples of those stressors include:

Competition: The pressure to win and outperform others can create additional stress.

Injury and Recovery: The fear of injury and the challenges of rehabilitation adds another layer of stress.

Public Scrutiny: Athletes, especially those in the public eye, must deal with the constant criticism and attention of social media.

Balancing Multiple Roles: Often, athletes must balance training, competitions, school, work, and personal relationships.

High Expectations: Both self-imposed and external expectations can lead to stress, particularly when the athlete feels they must always perform at their best.

While stress is inevitable, athletes need to learn how to overcome, manage, and cope with it. It will not be easy or instantaneous; it will be gradual. Sometimes, it will take losing multiple games or reassigning your training or support before realizing where and what causes stress.

Demystifying Stress and Pressure in Sports

What comes to mind when you hear the words stress and pressure?

Chances are you get a negative association with stress and pressure; however, it doesn't have to be. Stress and pressure in small amounts can be motivational and inspirational, helping the athlete actually excel (DiGiulio, 2023). It is for this reason that athletes, coaches, and parents understand the difference and know the fine line between healthy and unhealthy pressures.

The Fine Line Between Healthy and Unhealthy Pressures and Stress

What distinguishes healthy and unhealthy pressures and stress is how the athlete responds and reacts. An athlete with healthy pressures and stress will not feel overwhelmed or discouraged; in fact, they will use this time to reevaluate their goals, reassess, and discuss with their coaches or parents how to improve.

On the flip side, if an athlete is experiencing unhealthy pressures or stress, they will be short-tempered, easily frustrated or discouraged, and not enjoying the sport or activity. Typically, unhealthy pressures and stress motivate an athlete not to want to pursue any further competition or engagement in the sport. Two things can happen in this situation: the athlete can speak with someone and ask for tips and techniques for coping, or they can give up. Unfortunately, giving up is a route that athletes often embark on because, at this point, they are frustrated and feel discouraged (Thurott, 2023).

Destressing Techniques

To help with the unhealthy pressures and stress, here are a few things that can help to destress:

Deep Breathing: Helps calm the nervous system and reduce anxiety.

Visualization: Mentally rehearsing and visualizing your gameplay can boost confidence.

Progressive Muscle Relaxation: Reduces physical tension by systematically tensing and relaxing muscle groups.

Mindfulness Meditation: Encourages present-moment awareness, reducing the impact of stressors.

Physical Activity: Non-competitive physical activity can release endorphins and reduce stress.

Time Management: Prioritizing tasks and setting realistic goals can help reduce the stress of juggling multiple responsibilities.

Social Support: Talking to coaches, teammates, or a mental health professional can relieve emotions.

Of course, practicing visualization or engaging in deep breathing may be easy enough; what it will take is practice, patience, and consistency (DiGiulio, 2023).

Time Management and Stress

Athlete or not, time management is an important life skill because, without it, it can exacerbate undue stress. We often don't think about time management or training during competition, because an athlete's focus and concentration are directed at their one task—to win and perform.

How can an athlete practice time management?

Prioritizing Tasks: Focus on the most critical tasks and allocate time accordingly.

Creating a Schedule: Develop a daily or weekly schedule to manage all responsibilities.

Setting Realistic Goals: Break down larger goals into manageable steps to avoid feeling overwhelmed.

Just as an athlete may have a pre-game routine, creating a list of tasks or things to do will help alleviate stress and mitigate unexpected events. Why? Creating lists is one form of practicing time management, and lists are one form of accountability. Remember how visualization is one way of coping and building mental strength; this is what writing down a list can do and how it helps.

Resilience in Stress and Pressure

Bouncing back after a loss or injury will dictate an athlete's longevity in the sport, but more importantly, it will also demonstrate their mental strength. Demonstrating resilience amongst setbacks will help with the pressures and stress that athletes face regularly. A resilient mindset means you have a growth mindset, which means athletes are open to learning and growing. This is one thing that distinguishes successful athletes from those who are not.

Practicing resilience is also a way of demonstrating self-compassion, as we are our worst enemy and biggest competitor. Practicing self-compassion is one way of demonstrating resiliency during times of adversity.

Knowing Your Boundaries and Limits

But how do you know if you are practicing resiliency or experiencing stress?

Just as it is important to recognize the signs of stress, knowing your limits and boundaries is essential. Recognizing an athlete's limits and boundaries is a step towards preventing burnout and possibly injury. Boundary setting isn't always easy—this is where coaches, parents and teammates come into play. For example, an athlete who was previously injured and is now back competing would want to set their limits to having practices every other day, allowing rest and recovery. On top of creating boundaries, athletes should be able to create a balance between their training and personal life, which can drastically impact their mental mindset.

When athletes don't set their boundaries and limits, burnout is highly possible, and it can impact their long-term mindset to the point they may have a negative mindset towards the sport or training.

Rest, Recovery and Self Care

As discussed, boundaries and limits are essential, especially when it comes to recovery and resting, but it's also an important part of practicing self-care.

When it comes to rest, recovery, and self-care, athletes, along with their coaches and mentors, need to ensure that these are done regularly and with focus.

Rest

Allowing our body and mind to recover from the physical, mental, and emotional demands of training is important. Having adequate amounts of rest prevents the potential for burnout and reduces the likelihood of injury. It's important for athletes to be mindful and aware of the value of resting; without it, it could be a sign that one is pushing one's boundaries and limits.

Recovery

Often, we think that bouncing back from certain injuries will be quick and easy; however, if we don't give our bodies the time to rest and the proper recovery, a future injury is possible. Recovery, however, isn't just about injuries; it's about doing things to help your body repair and rebuild, such as staying hydrated, eating a healthy and balanced meal, and doing pre- and post-stretches. These are a few things athletes can do to aid in their recovery after a training or game.

Self-Care

Athletes face a lot of pressures, both internally and externally, which is why it is important to take proactive measures to mitigate any potential threats to our mental, physical, and emotional well-being. This is where self-care comes into play. Self-care is about putting one's needs first and foremost and recognizing when one needs to stop and take a step back. Often, not having a proper self-care routine can result in burnout.

Athletes need to remember this trifecta of rest, recovery and self-care. When not having even one of the three, athletes will notice a significant difference in their mental and emotional well-being. Balance is crucial, and professional athletes understand this. Sometimes, knowing one's limits or taking a pause is seen as a bad thing or weak—on the contrary, this takes courage, which is what athletes need to remember. There is nothing weak about focusing and putting your well-being first.

Ten Quick Tips for...

Athletes, coaches, and mentors have a lot on their plates, so here are a few tips to help in a pinch.

Stress-Busting

Are you feeling overwhelmed? Do you find yourself replaying negative self-talk? Do you think that your body and mind are disconnected?

Here are ten stress-busting tips to help you get centered and find your inner zen.

Practice Deep Breathing: A simple yet effective way to calm the mind.

Engage in Physical Activity: Exercise can be a powerful stress reliever, and it doesn't have to be in the sport you play—it can be just going for walk.

Stay Organized: Use planners or apps to keep track of tasks and deadlines; time management can help alleviate and mitigate stressful situations.

Get Enough Sleep: Aim for 7–9 hours of quality sleep per night.

Eat a Balanced Diet: Proper nutrition supports both physical and mental health.

Stay Hydrated: Dehydration can increase stress levels, and drinking water or high-electrolyte drinks can help counter this (Harlo Staff, 2024).

Practice Gratitude: Focus on the positive to shift the mindset.

Take Breaks: Regular breaks prevent burnout and maintain focus.

Connect With Loved Ones: Social (friends, family, coaches) support is crucial for emotional well-being.

Seek Professional Help: Consult a mental health professional if stress becomes overwhelming.

Pressure Mantras

When we need to redirect the thoughts of self-doubt, fear and insecurity—here are ten mantras to remember to help you overcome those invasive and hindering thoughts.

"I am prepared for this moment."

"Pressure is a privilege."

"I focus on what I can control."

"Every challenge is an opportunity."

"I trust in my training."

"I breathe in calmness; I breathe out tension."

"I am resilient and strong."

"Mistakes are a part of growth."

"I stay present in the moment."

"I perform with confidence and ease."

Chapter 7:

The Resilient Athlete

> *I know fear is an obstacle for some people, but it is an illusion to me. Failure always made me try harder the next time.* –Michael Jordan

Resiliency is a trait that differentiates successful athletes from those who struggle under pressure. Having the ability to bounce back from adversity while still maintaining focus and moving forward is an invaluable and key skill set for athletes who want to thrive and succeed. Often, the association with resiliency in sports is physical, but it is also about the mental and emotional bounce back that matters and counts. An athlete can bounce back and demonstrate resilience physically; however, if they cannot get back into the zone or focus mentally, their athletic performance will be hindered.

Consider the following scenario...

Sam is an athlete who recognizes the pressure in front of him before a big game. Rather than allowing the pressure of the match to bog him down, he takes a deep breath and remembers all the time he's spent preparing for this moment. Sam knows that if he doesn't make the shot, it's okay because there is still plenty of time left to bounce back, and if they lose, there's always a next game to improve and get better.

In this scenario, Sam remains composed and demonstrates mental toughness. He's using the knowledge and experience that, win or lose, there is an opportunity to grow and improve for next time.

Here's another scenario with athlete Jenna...

Jenna hears the gym fill with boos and taunts. She becomes overwhelmed by the outside noise and begins overthinking and doubting herself. She knows if they miss the shot, everyone will be disappointed in her, and she will question whether she should be playing at all. She misses the shot, and even though her team says she tried, she can't help but feel responsible for the loss.

While Sam had the mental capabilities to shift his mindset and trust in himself, Jenna did not. She doubted herself and was unable to redirect the negative self-talk. She also assumed the pressure of her teammates despite them encouraging and providing emotional and moral support. Not having the ability to demonstrate resilience, Jenna began a downward mental and emotional spiral that affected her confidence, performance, and team dynamic.

In both cases, each athlete found themselves in high-pressure and stressful situations; however, how they managed them was very different. One demonstrated resilience, while the other did not. This shows that mental toughness and resilience will allow an athlete to cope with and manage stress and pressure and see each opportunity as learning and growing (Sutton, 2024).

The non-resilient athlete struggled to control the negative narrative that their mind and insecurities were fueling. As mentioned, this can deter athletes from continuing to play the sport if they feel overwhelmed or unable to cope with and manage the pressure and stress.

What Makes a Resilient Athlete

Various intrinsic and extrinsic factors make an athlete resilient. The combination of the two creates the ideal athlete who can manage and handle the pressures on and off the field.

Five factors distinguish a resilient athlete from others: mental toughness, support systems, experience with adversity, positive mindset, and motivation (Gupta & McCarthy, 2022).

Concentrating and staying focused while maintaining composure is a sign of mental toughness. Pushing through when every fiber in their body and mind says to quit, but they choose not to is a sign of a mentally strong mindset.

Having the mental strength and toughness to keep on with the journey also requires having a support system. This is why coaches, parents, and mentors need to be on the same level of understanding as their athletes. If there is a disconnect between an athlete and their support system, whether in their goals or values, an athlete will struggle to bounce back and adapt in the face of challenges.

Athletes, competitive or not, are well-versed in challenges, and resilient people see these challenges as stepping stones along their journey to their ultimate goal (Gupta & McCarthy, 2022). Athletes who embrace these situations rather than dwell on them and allow them to hold them back are likelier to succeed and excel.

How Does Resilience Play Into Sports?

Mental strength, gamesmanship, and leadership are essential to sports, and resiliency is crucial. Resiliency is an integral part of an athlete's success as it touches on all aspects of their training, performance, development, and growth into a well-rounded athlete.

Athletes who can focus and drown out distractions, whether on or off the field, display mental strength, which is crucial in high-stakes situations.

We will discuss it later, but even in individual sports, there is still a team, and resilient athletes understand that their success is not just their own but a combination of the support and encouragement of others. It's not just those who play on the same team but opponents and competitors can inspire resiliency, as gamesmanship demonstrates growth and maturity for an athlete.

Resilience on the Court

On the court, resilience can be shown through actions and behaviors. Five ways that athletes demonstrate resilience on the court or field are:

1. **Focus**: Maintaining their concentration during a high-stress moment, such as a playoff game or a penalty shot, will allow them to embrace the outcome and grow from it, regardless of what it is.

2. **Positive Self-Talk**: Positive affirmation and self-encouragement can help athletes stay confident and sure of their training. Athletes need to be able to mentally get in the zone themselves and not just rely on others to get them to a certain level of confidence.

3. **Adaptability**: Being flexible and adaptable during gameplay means an athlete can go with the flow. Athletes who can't adapt or struggle will not be able to succeed and thrive, as they will also follow a rigid mindset.

4. **Managing Mistakes**: While we may wish to make every shot we take, the reality is that there will be times we miss shots, but what matters is how we move forward and onward. Being resilient means not letting mistakes that happened affect the rest of the game—in the words of Taylor Swift, it's important to "shake it off".

5. **Consistency**: Consistent training and communication mean that whatever happens, an athlete can trust and have faith in their abilities. If an athlete does not train regularly or is not consistent in their technique, then there is a chance they may fail.

Resilience off the Court

Just because a game is over does not mean practicing resiliency stops. Resiliency can be practiced and continued off the court, and it matters just as much.

Here are five ways athletes can practice resiliency off the court.

1. **Mindfulness and Meditation**: Mindfulness and meditation can promote stress management and create a balanced mindset. They can also help athletes decompress after a game.

2. **Physical Training:** Consistency is key; therefore, regular training is important. This does not mean that training should only happen during the season; it should also be continued off-season. Doing this will build physical and mental endurance.

3. **Learning From Setbacks**: Reflecting on past setbacks, such as losses, and understanding what can be improved or changed is one way of practicing resiliency.

4. **Maintaining a Support Network**: Athletes' relationships should be well-versed in more than just the sport itself. A well-rounded athlete will have a support network that includes their coaches, friends, and family, who can be their sounding board and cheerleader.

5. **Goal-Setting**: It is not enough to have goals on the court; it's important also to have goals that athletes can work toward that touch their personal, professional, and academic lives.

Achieving a Resilient Mindset

The biggest thing that athletes need to remember, whether training or achieving resiliency, is that consistency is key. Without consistency, the foundation is built on unstable ground, and the naturalness of having our mind adapt to and manage high-pressure situations is lost or nonexistent.

Characteristics of a Resilient Athlete

All resilient athletes possess five characteristics: optimism, perseverance, emotional regulation, self-discipline and adaptability (Gupta & McCarthy, 2022).

Optimism: Regardless of the outcome, resilient athletes maintain a positive outlook despite setbacks. Athletes believe in their ability to overcome and grow from the challenges they experience.

Perseverance: Being able to persevere in the face of adversity is more than a trait; it's a superpower. Perseverance demonstrates an athlete's unyielding determination not to give up and to continue.

Emotional Regulation: Managing emotions, especially during a high-pressure situation, is a key component of resilience. Resilient athletes can remain calm and focused even if chaos ensues around them.

Self-Discipline: Resilient athletes are able to maintain focus and discipline regardless of outside influences and factors. They understand the importance of training or being focused, so they know that commitment is part of achieving their goals.

Adaptability: All athletes know that anything can happen during a game. Therefore, adaptability is a key component of resilience. Changing circumstances can include injury or environmental; an athlete who can roll with the punches is likelier to thrive rather than struggle in the face of adversity.

All resilient athletes demonstrate these five traits, which distinguish a mentally tough athlete from one who is not.

Overcoming the Setbacks and Bouncing Back

In the world of sports, setbacks are inevitable and part of the reality of being an athlete. Whether it's a loss or injury, how an athlete responds to these challenges is a test of their resilience.

Bouncing back involves a process of mental, emotional, and physical recovery. Resilient athletes always view setbacks as invaluable learning opportunities that help them grow and develop. Mentally, shifting to a growth mindset will allow an athlete to not see losses or adversity as a hindrance. This is why resiliency is often associated with a growth mindset. Athletes who take adversities and perceive them as opportunities recognize they have shortfalls and want to improve, so they develop a mindset that will embrace rather than be hindered.

Quiz Time: Am I Resilient?

1. When you experience a setback or failure, you:

    a) Feel defeated and take a long time to recover
    b) Feel discouraged but eventually move on
    c) Quickly analyze what went wrong and bounce back

2. How do you handle unexpected training or competition schedule changes?

    a) Get frustrated and struggle to adapt
    b) Feel unsettled but try to adjust
    c) Remain flexible and adapt quickly

3. When you face a challenging opponent, you:

    a) Doubt your abilities and feel overwhelmed
    b) Feel anxious but try to rise to the challenge
    c) Embrace the challenge and stay confident in your abilities

4. How do you respond to criticism from coaches or teammates?

    a) Take it personally and feel disheartened
    b) Reflect on it and try to improve
    c) Use it constructively to fuel your improvement

5. When you're feeling physically or mentally exhausted, you:

    a) Find it hard to push through and often give up
    b) Struggle but try to keep going
    c) Dig deep and push through the fatigue

6. How do you set goals after a major setback or injury?

    a) Avoid setting new goals for fear of failing again
    b) Set goals but with caution and some hesitation
    c) Set new, realistic goals and stay motivated to achieve them

7. During a competition, if you fall behind, you:

    a) Feel defeated and lose motivation
    b) Feel stressed but try to catch up
    c) Stay focused and work harder to turn the situation around

8. How do you deal with long-term pressure and stress from your sport?

    a) Feel overwhelmed and consider quitting
    b) Struggle but find ways to cope
    c) Manage stress effectively and use it to stay motivated

Analyzing Your Results

Mostly A's: Low Resilience

You might struggle with bouncing back from setbacks and adapting to challenges. Building resilience through mental training, positive self-talk, and seeking support can help you become more resilient.

Mostly B's: Moderate Resilience

You have a moderate level of resilience and can handle some challenges. Strengthening your coping strategies and maintaining a positive mindset can help you become more resilient.

Mostly C's: High Resilience

You demonstrate high resilience and can effectively bounce back from setbacks. Continue to leverage your positive mindset, adaptability, and determination to maintain and build on your resilience.

Chapter 8:

Teamwork: How to Thrive as a Team Player

Talent wins games, but teamwork and intelligence win championships.
–Michael Jordan

Success is rarely achieved alone; therefore, the saying, "There is no 'I' in team," is a perfect truth for athletes to not only know but embrace. A team is behind the star athlete even in solo sports such as tennis, track or golf. This team can include coaches, mentors, trainers, and family, all working to do what they can to help their athletes succeed.

There's No "I" in Team

The sentence, "There's no 'I' in team," reminds us that success on and off the field results from a collective effort (Hicks, 2024). A network of individuals guides, mentors, and supports the athletes in their endeavors. When it comes to athletes who play individual sports, it can be hard to see how there is a team, especially if the athlete is relying on their training and skills, but one has to remember that the athlete has a team of people supporting their training efforts. Someone has been guiding and mentoring them—from providing feedback on their technique to encouraging them.

While it's essential to recognize that there is a team behind every athlete, it's just as important to acknowledge the struggles and barriers that an athlete can face. When you have a team, there is a delicate balance between communicating effectively and managing all the goals and expectations of every part of the team.

How can you balance individual and team goals and expectations?

At the end of the day, regardless of the other goals and expectations, the ultimate goal is to succeed, and by using this common goal, athletes and their teammates can work towards achieving it collectively.

Teamwork Makes the Dream Work

A strong team fosters collaboration, communication and a shared commitment toward a goal.

Consider the following traits of teamwork and what they look like in a cohesive versus a non-cohesive team.

Trait	Cohesive Team	Non-Cohesive Team
Communication	Open, honest and clear	Misunderstanding and jumping to conclusions
Trust	High level of trust	Low trust, results in suspicion
Shared Goal	Unified and agreed-upon common end goal	Conflicting personal aspirations
Support	Support and encourage each other	Internal competition, everyone looks out for themselves
Accountability	Everyone takes responsibility for their actions and behaviors	Blame shifting—not owning up to their actions
Respect	Mutual respect amongst all individuals, whether they are on their team or not	Disrespect and undermining teammates

| Adaptability | Willingness and openness to adapt to change and unexpected situations | Resistance to change |

When a non-cohesive team displays these traits, it can lead to a breakdown in cooperation and engagement. This can happen not only on the court but also off the court. Conversely, a cohesive team that displays these traits is more likely to succeed and is open to ensuring everyone succeeds.

When an athlete transitions from solo to team sports, this shift can require adjustments to their mindset. Embracing these traits of cohesion, both from the athlete and the team itself, will help ensure everyone is on the same page and focused on the same goal.

Along with possessing and practicing these traits within a team, empathy and compassion are also important.

Practicing Empathy and Compassion

Why are empathy and compassion important for athletes? The ability to understand and share feelings and do what one can to help alleviate discomfort demonstrates mental strength (Bergin, 2020). When athletes can set aside their own needs and demonstrate selflessness, they show a strength of adaptability and, more importantly, empathy and compassion, creating a positive and supportive environment.

What does empathy and compassion look like in sports?

Aspect	On the Field	Off the Field
Empathy in Sports	A player notices a teammate is struggling and offers encouragement and support.	A player recognizes the stress a teammate is under and offers to help with practice or personal issues.

Compassion in Sports	A player helps an injured opponent, showing that sportsmanship goes beyond winning and sides.	A team organizes a fundraiser for a teammate or community initiative
Lack of Empathy and Compassion	A player ignores a teammate's struggle or uses their mistakes to boost their own position.	A lack of support for teammates' personal issues leads to division amongst the team.

A team or athlete that practices and advocates empathy and compassion is more cohesive and more resilient. There is also less chance of internal conflicts and unhealthy internal competition.

Becoming a Leader On and Off the Field

When athletes demonstrate empathy and compassion, they are subtly demonstrating leadership. Being a leader in sports is not about being the loudest or dominant on and off the field; instead, it's about setting an example, taking responsibility, and helping others achieve their personal best. At times, athletes demonstrate these qualities without realizing the positive impact they are having—this is what makes them natural leaders.

Leaders thrive and succeed because of their mental strength and ability to rise to the challenge during difficult situations. They also don't tend to be the star player, not because they can't, but because they genuinely thrive on ensuring everyone can demonstrate their skillset.

Balancing Leadership With Individuality

While an athlete who demonstrates leadership traits doesn't just aim to be the star, there is a delicate balance between leading and losing focus on their goals and individuality. It can be a balancing act between the two, especially regarding personal and team goals.

The only way to achieve this balance is through trial and error, open communication, and honesty. If an athlete can be transparent and state what they want to work toward but also recognize the team's needs, they can mutually work towards their goals and not lose sight of their individuality.

Leadership, whether blatantly visible or not, plays an important role in guiding a team through the challenges of their sport, both on and off the field. It's not just an athlete's talent that leads to victory; it's also the encouragement of a parent and the mentoring of a coach—all these and more lead to success. By remembering their common goal, an athlete and a team are working towards that goal and using everyone's strengths.

Navigating Conflict

Common Conflicts in Sports and Team Play

Think of some of the biggest names in sports and how often we see headlines about their competition or feud. In hockey, there are the Toronto Maple Leafs and the Boston Bruins; in soccer, there's Manchester United and Liverpool; these are teams where conflict and competition are part of the game.

The one thing that differentiates this situation from everyday situations is that most of these athletes are able to talk together and have mutual respect for their competition because they have mentally trained themselves to recognize competition as a form of growth.

Conflict Resolution Techniques

With so many players involved in a game's victories, conflict is inevitable; however, there are ways to mitigate, if not minimize, the likelihood of conflict.

Here are a few conflict resolution techniques to help athletes and their teammates.

Open Dialogue: Open communication and transparency.

Active Listening: Making all parties feel heard and understood can mitigate any misunderstanding.

Compromise and Collaboration: Finding a common middle ground works to ensure everyone feels they have a stake.

Mediation: Having a neutral third party to facilitate or be part of discussions can help get a perspective that may not always be apparent.

Boundaries: Setting clear boundaries, such as when to have discussions, what's acceptable, etc., can help prevent escalation in conflict.

When these techniques are used, they can help resolve conflict and strengthen the relationships and communication among athletes and team players. Having a unified front and wanting to find productive ways of problem-solving will further develop a growth mindset and resiliency in you as an athlete and within the team dynamics.

Quiz Time: Am I a Team Player?

1. When working on a project or task, you prefer to:

    a) Collaborate with others and share ideas
    b) Work independently and rely on your skills

2. In a competitive situation, you feel most motivated by:

    a) The success of the entire team
    b) Your achievements and performance

3. How do you handle responsibilities and roles within a group?

    a) Enjoy taking on roles that support the team's goals
    b) Prefer to take on tasks that highlight your strengths

4. When receiving feedback, you:

    a) Appreciate feedback that benefits the team's overall performance
    b) Value feedback that focuses on your improvement

5. In practice sessions, you:

    a) Thrive on drills and activities that involve teamwork
    b) Prefer exercises that allow you to focus on your skills

6. How do you feel about sharing credit for success?

    a) Feel proud to share the success with your teammates
    b) Prefer to receive individual recognition for your contributions

7. When facing a challenge, you:

    a) Seek support and input from your team
    b) Rely on your own strategies and solutions

8. Your ideal training environment is:

    a) One where teamwork and group activities are emphasized
    b) One where you can focus on your personal goals and progress

9. In a leadership role, you:

    a) Focus on motivating and bringing out the best in your team
    b) Lead by example, showcasing your skills and dedication

10. How do you celebrate victories?

    a) With your team, valuing the collective effort
    b) By reflecting on your performance and contributions

Analyzing Your Results

Mostly A's: Team Player

You thrive in collaborative environments and enjoy working with others to achieve common goals. You value teamwork, collective effort, and group success.

Mostly B's: Individual Player

You excel in settings where you can focus on your personal skills and achievements. You prefer to rely on your abilities and take pride in individual accomplishments.

Chapter 9:

The Balancing Act: School, Life and Sports

Life is a balancing act between getting ahead and getting along.
–Dr. Paul T.P. Wong

Athletes wear many different hats. These hats represent the various roles in their day-to-day lives, from student to teammate to sibling to friend. However, unlike the average person, athletes can often struggle to juggle these hats, especially when it comes to high-pressure situations that may conflict with their other roles. As a result, balancing being an athlete with everything else can prove difficult but very possible.

Juggling Our Many Hats

Athletes embody several identities, each with their own set of unique expectations and responsibilities.

Typical hats that athletes wear include:

Hat	Expectation
Student	Manage their academic responsibilities with training.
Athlete	Focus on their training, performance and skill development, and ensure they are always at their peak.

Teammate	Maintain and build relationships within the team, collaborate with others and contribute to the common goal of winning.
Friend	Maintain and foster social connections outside of sports.
Family	Fulfil familial obligations and expectations.

While we would like to believe that these roles will flawlessly align and mesh together, they don't always. The time and effort required for being a student will differ from the time and effort needed for the role of friend or family member (Mottern, 2023). There will be times when the roles that an athlete plays will conflict with one another; this conflict can sometimes result in stress and anxiety.

The Struggle to Embracing Multiple Identities

It can be an emotional and mental challenge to embrace and separate the various roles an athlete possesses; sometimes, this struggle expresses itself on the field as anxiety and overwhelm. It can also manifest itself as burnout and strained relationships. Athletes who are able to maintain the multiple identities and relationships associated with each one do so because they have not only prioritized their goals but have aligned them with their roles, therefore striking that balance that enables them to bounce from one role to another without stress, anxiety and frustration.

For example, an athlete who aspires to become a doctor knows the importance of her academics. Still, they also know their team has an important game coming up and will need to ensure they get extra training sessions. If athletes do not have coping skills such as time management, they will feel overwhelmed and could potentially shut down. The failure to truly integrate the multiple identities can not only result in anxiety and a sense of being overwhelmed, but it can also impact their own perception of self. The identity confusion could make them question whether or not they are living up to their expectations, if they are actually happy or if this is worth the worries and struggle. An internal conflict like this can distract and create a mind block that prevents them from being able to perform at their best.

Wearing Your Hat With Pride

Being an athlete is something to be proud of in and of itself; however, the other identities and associated roles also need to be worn with pride. Embodying the various identities will strengthen one's ability to shift and adapt mentally. Having this level of self-awareness allows an athlete to feel empowered and confident.

Similar to how an athlete feels accomplished and proud when scoring that winning goal, knowing that they can be star athletes and students is also something they can be proud of. Why? Because it fuels their confidence and enhances their life and purpose by demonstrating to themselves that they are capable of not only performing under pressure but also ensuring that other aspects of their lives are prosperous and thriving as well. Being a student-athlete is a testament to one's ability when it comes to balancing academics and sports, showcasing discipline, time management, and perseverance. Similarly, being a supportive teammate or a caring friend highlights empathy, cooperation, and emotional intelligence.

How to Balance Sports and Life

The delicate balance between sports and other aspects of an athlete's life will require the athlete to recognize the short, medium, and long-term struggles and, after identifying them, understand the effort and demands needed to address the challenges.

Let's look at the matrix of student and athlete and the challenges one could face.

	Student	Athlete
Daily	Attending classes, completing assignments, studying for exams, managing time, and staying organized.	Training sessions, physical conditioning, skill development, injury prevention, and maintaining focus.
Weekly	Preparing for exams, participating in group projects, attending extracurricular activities, and socializing with peers.	Competition, recovering from injury, analyzing performance, and maintaining motivation.
Monthly	Meeting academic deadlines, dealing with exams or major projects, planning for future semesters, and managing stress.	Seasonal peaks in competition, adjusting training regimens, handling travel for away games, and coping with pressure.

When we have situations where an athlete's roles intersect, expectations and responsibilities increase, which can negatively impact an athlete's mental, emotional, and physical well-being (Mottern, 2023). To avoid this potential overload, an athlete needs to find ways of creating a balance.

Ways to Create Balance

As with everything, balance is important. The struggle with trying to achieve that balance is knowing what to achieve and how to achieve it.

Here are a few tips on how athletes can create a balance between their roles and their expectations:

Time Management: Creating schedules and prioritizing things based on importance.

Boundary Setting: Saying "no" is not always easy; however, when you can learn to confidently say no to things that either have no value or detract from your goals, you are creating a balance by setting a boundary.

Support: Athletes have a team behind them, from coaches to mentors, teachers, and family and friends, and they must take advantage of them. It's even more important they seek support before they reach burnout.

Mindfulness: From deep breathing to meditation, incorporating mindfulness into one's day-to-day routine will help strike that balance of expectation and calmness. It is also a great technique for reducing stress.

Balance Through Goals

Knowing our goals and priorities will be crucial in an athlete's journey to striking a balance because they provide direction and motivation. When an athlete has neither, the pendulum can be imbalanced, and the athlete can find themselves easily overwhelmed and lacking in direction. Having direction and purpose is an aspect of mental preparedness and strength that athletes and non-athletes should strive for (Feigley, 2018). What happens when a goal is accomplished? Remember, they are not static; they are evolving, just as an athlete's priorities, goals and expectations evolve.

Don't Forget Self-Care

It can't be stressed enough that maintaining various roles and expectations is mentally exhausting; therefore, practicing self-care will be important in preventing and mitigating burnout and mental fatigue (Feigley, 2018). Often, we perceive self-care as just taking a mental break; however, it is also about ensuring a healthy and balanced diet, prioritizing rest, and recognizing the signs of stress. Being able to practice self-care is about having a self-awareness of what their body and mind are telling them. Ignoring these signs can prove useless if one wants to be the best—as all the great athletes know the value and importance of self-care.

Balancing Relationships

It is natural that with each identity, there are different relationships an athlete must also manage. Whether it is a teammate, friend, family member, or coach, these relationships will not only foster a healthy, positive environment and balance, but they are also a way of maintaining positive relationships.

Balancing Teammates and Friendships

Given that athletes spend significant time with their teammates, this can lead to strong bonds. However, it is just as essential to maintain their friendships outside of sports as well. Not doing so can sometimes result in conflict; signs of conflict between these relationships might include feelings of neglect or jealousy (Carpentier, 2023). To embrace both types of relationships, athletes must maintain open lines of communication, make a conscious effort to make time for both groups and respect each relationship dynamic and their needs.

Creating a Circle of Support and Encouragement

A support circle consists of individuals offering encouragement, guidance, and positivity. This can include coaches, mentors, friends, and family. When athletes surround themselves with supportive people, it can boost their confidence, provide motivation, and help them navigate challenges by using them as a sounding board or simply just support.

What does encouragement look like? It can take many forms, such as verbal praise, positive reinforcement, or simply showing up. On the flip side, a lack of encouragement might involve criticism, negativity, or indifference. By fostering a circle of support, athletes create an environment where they can thrive on and off the field (Carpentier, 2023).

Navigating Social Challenges and Pressures

If the pressures of juggling relationships are not enough, athletes can also face various social challenges and pressures.

These challenges might include:

Fitting In: The pressure to conform to social norms or be part of the "in crowd" can be challenging, yet it's an expectation they face. To not feel the pressures and embrace their authentic self, whatever that may be, athletes need to stay true to their values and identity, even when it means standing apart or being on the outside of the "norm."

Performance Pressure: The expectation to perform well can lead to stress and anxiety. This pressure may come from coaches, teammates, or self-imposed expectations.

Balancing Academics and Sports: The need to excel in both areas can create stress and time constraints, leading to burnout if not managed properly.

Social Media: The pressure to maintain a particular image online can add to the stress of being an athlete, leading to issues with body image, self-worth and an athlete's overall sense of self (Huber, 2023).

Conflict Within Relationship (Friends or Family): Balancing the demands of sports with relationships can create tension, especially if friends or family feel neglected.

When athletes start to recognize these challenges, they can utilize their coping skills and develop strategies to address and mitigate them.

Putting You First

With so many pressures and challenges, athletes must prioritize themselves and their well-being. This means putting mental health, physical health, and personal happiness first. It's not the people on the sidelines who have to perform or make the shot, it's YOU, the athlete, so remembering that you matter and you know yourself better than anyone is going to be important in having a mentally strong and confident mindset.

Conclusion: The Road Ahead

We've explored the various factors, traits, and skillsets needed to grow and develop mental strength and resilience. Becoming a top-tier athlete is not a straight and easy-cut journey; instead, it's a roller coaster of highs and lows. There will be victories and losses, but what will separate athletes is their resilience and mental capability to thrive. Mental toughness was never just about overcoming obstacles; it was and is about an athlete's ability to demonstrate resilience, humility, grace, patience and compassion.

Success and confidence don't happen overnight. The cliche saying "practice makes perfect" is a fundamental truth for any athlete looking to be the best. Every drill, practice, and game contributes not just to an athlete's capabilities but also to their mental strength. This relentless pursuit of greatness and winning is just a tiny part of what distinguishes athletes from focused, goal-oriented ones.

Following Your Passion

When you fuel the fire within, that determination and drive will always guide you to stay on the course to being mentally strong and capable. Remember the highs and lows? When you pursue your passion, the lows will always be seen as a stepping stone to fulfilling your athletic dreams and goals. Even in losses and adversity, passion and determination will always trump. Whether you are leading a team or a solo athlete, wearing the letter C for captain or are an unspoken leader—when you have pursued your passion on the field, the struggle of performance anxiety or pressures is never embraced as a hardship; instead, it is embraced as a learning and growing moment.

That growth mindset will and continues to help athletes excel. Even if they don't make it to the NHL or NBA, a growth mindset and mental toughness will always benefit them.

Will your passion change?

Will your outlook on the game and your goals change?

Most likely—but if you have planned and trained to be adaptable, the journey toward mental strength will serve you well!

Remember, just because you finished this book does not mean you cannot go back through the chapters to check in and get a pulse on your communication or leadership style. The journey to becoming a star athlete is an evolution, so it is important to be aware and do a pulse check on how you are evolving, as the last thing you want is to take a step back in your growth and development.

References

Ardent Financial. (2022, August 10). *3 powerful lessons long-distance running can teach investors*. https://ardentuk.com/news/3-powerful-lessons-long-distance-running-can-teach-investors/

Armstrong, T. (2023, August 31). *Parenting in youth sports – the good, the not so good, and the ugly*. CASEM/ACMSE. https://www.casem-acmse.org/news/parenting-in-youth-sports/

Ashe, D. (2020). *Arthur Ashe quotes*. Bradford Grammar School Blog. https://bgslearning.wordpress.com/2020/02/24/success-is-a-journey-arthur-ashe/

Barman, D. D. (2023, September 18). *From Williams sisters to Kylian Mbappé, 10 athletes who were coached by their fathers*. Market Realist. https://marketrealist.com/10-athletes-who-were-coached-by-their-fathers/

Baxter-Jones, A. D. G., & Maffulli, N. (2003). Parental influence on sport participation in elite young athletes, *Journal of Sports Medicine and Physical Fitness, 43*(2), 250–255. https://www.proquest.com/openview/5f4723c316971b900a0f936fd78df7e7/1?pq-origsite=gscholar&cbl=4718

Bergin, M. S. (2020). *Teen sports: Risks and rewards*. Y Magazine. https://magazine.byu.edu/article/teen-sports-can-build-empathy-resilience-and-relationships/

Brenner, J. S. (2023). Mindfulness for young athletes. *Sports Health: A Multidisciplinary Approach, 16*(2). https://doi.org/10.1177/19417381231209219

Bryant, K. (2018). *The Mamba Mentality: How I play*. MCD, Farrar, Strauss, and Giroux.

Carpentier, M. (2023, February 9). *Sports and friendships go hand-in-hand*. FHC Sports Report. https://fhcsportsreport.com/21175/columns/sports-and-friendships-go-hand-in-hand/

Carter, P. (2020, March 10). *Council post: Mamba mentality: The mindset it takes to be the best.* Forbes. https://www.forbes.com/sites/forbescoachescouncil/2020/03/10/mamba-mentality-the-mindset-it-takes-to-be-the-best/

Cohn, P. J. (2018, March 26). *7 STRATEGIES TO HELP YOUR ATHLETE BE MORE CONFIDENT.* Blue Star Lacrosse. https://www.bluestarlacrosse.com/news_article/show/727837-7-strategies-to-help-your-athlete-be-more-confident

Condor Performance. (2020, June 22). *Here are some of the best sport psychology quotes ever.* Condor Performance. https://condorperformance.com/best-sport-psychology-quotes/

Dealing with distraction. (2021, February 26). Prepared Athlete Training & Health. https://preparedathlete.info/prepared-blog/dealing-with-distraction

DiGiulio, M. (2023, April 10). *The effects of stress on your athletic performance.* Performance. https://www.performanceorthosports.com/blog/the-effects-of-stress-on-your-athletic-performance-35642.html

Doran, G. (1981). There's a S.M.A.R.T. way to write management's goals and objectives. *Management Review, 70, 35-36.* https://www.scirp.org/reference/ReferencesPapers?ReferenceID=1459599

Federer, R. (n.d.). *20 Roger Federer quotes.* Mirror Review Quotes. https://quotes.mirrorreview.com/roger-federer-quotes-igniting-sportsmanship/

Feigley, D. (2018). *Effective goal setting for youth sports.* Rutgers University Youth Sports Research. https://youthsports.rutgers.edu/wp-content/uploads/Goal-Setting.pdf

Freeland, G. (2018, June 1). *Talent wins games, teamwork wins championships.* Forbes. https://www.forbes.com/sites/grantfreeland/2018/06/01/talent-wins-games-teamwork-wins-championships/#

G, A. (2013, November 6). *The parent-coach/child-athlete relationship in youth sport: Cordial, contentious, or conundrum?* Youth Development through Recreation and Sport; Youth Development Through Recreation and Sport. https://youthdevelopmentthrurecreation.wordpress.com/2013/11/06/the-parent-coachchild-athlete-relationship-in-youth-sport-cordial-contentious-or-conundrum-2/

Gupta, S., & McCarthy, P. J. (2022). The sporting resilience model: A systematic review of resilience in sport performers. *Frontiers in Psychology, 13*. https://doi.org/10.3389/fpsyg.2022.1003053

Harlo Staff. (2024, March 22). *The equilibrium of calm: Electrolyte balance in stress management*. Drink Harlo. https://drinkharlo.com/blogs/articles/the-equilibrium-of-calm-electrolyte-balance-in-stress-management?

Hicks, S. (2024, March 27). *Mental toughness in individual vs. team sports: Navigating the unique challenges*. Linkedin. https://www.linkedin.com/pulse/mental-toughness-individual-vs-team-sports-navigating-sa-quan-hicks-aw0ve/

Huber, B. (2023). *Negative social media and its influence on athlete's performance* [Master's thesis, California State Polytechnic University]. Humboldt Digital Commons. https://digitalcommons.humboldt.edu/cgi/viewcontent.cgi?article=1725&context=etd#

Jones, G., Hanton, S., & Connaughton, D. (2002). What is this thing called mental toughness? An investigation of elite sport performers. *Journal of Applied Sport Psychology, 14*(3), 205–218. https://doi.org/10.1080/10413200290103509

Jordan, M. (2019). MICHAEL JORDAN QUOTES. Goodreads.com. https://www.goodreads.com/quotes/45899-talent-wins-games-but-teamwork-and-intelligence-wins-championships

Kim, S., Park, S., Love, A., & Pang, T. C. (2021). Coaching style, sport enjoyment, and intent to continue participation among artistic swimmers. *International Journal of Sports Science & Coaching, 16*(3). https://doi.org/10.1177/1747954120984054

Knight, B. (2024). *Bobby Knight quotes*. Goodreads.com. https://www.goodreads.com/author/quotes/96179.Bobby_Knight

Lalonde, J. M. (2019, May 10). *Finding opportunity after failure: Is there always a bigger door?* The Wealthy Trainer. https://www.thewealthytrainer.com/post/when-a-door-slams-another-opens

Liddle, R. (2022, September 20). *"Success is a journey, not a destination..."* Savance Workplace. https://www.savanceworkplace.com/blog/success-is-a-journey-not-a-destination/

Locke, E. A., & Latham, G. P. (1990, April). *A theory of goal setting & task performance*. ResearchGate. https://www.researchgate.net/publication/232501090_A_Theory_of_Goal_Setting_Task_Performance

Monsma, E. V. (2018). *Principles of effective goal setting*. Association for Applied Sport Psychology. https://appliedsportpsych.org/resources/resources-for-athletes/principles-of-effective-goal-setting/

Mottern, C. (2023, June 2). *How to balance academic and athletic demands*. SportsEngine. https://discover.sportsengineplay.com/article/volleyball/how-balance-academic-and-athletic-demands

Murray, R. M., Dugdale, J. H., Habeeb, C. M., & Arthur, C. A. (2020). Transformational parenting and coaching on mental toughness and physical performance in adolescent soccer players: The moderating effect of athlete age. *European Journal of Sport Science*, 1–10. https://doi.org/10.1080/17461391.2020.1765027

Nadal, R. (2023). RAFAEL NADAL QUOTES. Goodreads.com. https://www.goodreads.com/quotes/9524329-losing-is-not-my-enemy-fear-of-losing-is-my-enemy

O'Rourke, D. J., Smith, R. E., Smoll, F. L., & Cumming, S. P. (2011). Trait anxiety in young athletes as a function of parental pressure and motivational climate: Is parental pressure always harmful? *Journal of*

Applied Sport Psychology, 23(4), 398–412. https://doi.org/10.1080/10413200.2011.552089

Ring, C., Whitehead, J., Gürpınar, B., & Kavussanu, M. (2023). Sport values, personal values and antisocial behavior in sport. *Sport Values, Personal Values and Antisocial Behavior in Sport.* https://doi.org/10.1016/j.ajsep.2023.05.002

Ryan, R. M., & Deci, E. L. (2000). Self-determination theory and the facilitation of intrinsic motivation, social development, and well-being. *American Psychologist, 55*(1), 68–78. https://selfdeterminationtheory.org/SDT/documents/2000_RyanDeci_SDT.pdf

Schwarzenegger, A. (2019). *Arnold Schwarzenegger quotes.* Challenge Achieved. https://www.challengeachieved.com/quote/strength-does-not-come-from-winning-your-5a804e13a45259477d4ee2b3

Siegfried, T. (2024, February 25). *The psychological coping mechanisms of elite athletes can help everyone face high-pressure situations.* Inverse. https://www.inverse.com/science/psychological-coping-mechanisms-elite-athletes

Straw, E. (2023, November 10). *Mindfulness: The key to improving focus as an athlete.* Success Starts Within. https://www.successstartswithin.com/sports-psychology-articles/mindfulness-training-for-athletes/mindfulness-the-key-to-improving-focus-as-an-athlete/

Sullivan, G. S., & Strode, J. P. (2010). Motivation through goal setting: A self-determined perspective. *Strategies, 23*(6), 18–23. https://doi.org/10.1080/08924562.2010.10590899

Sutton, J. (2024, April 1). *Boosting mental toughness in young athletes & 20 strategies.* PositivePsychology.com. https://positivepsychology.com/mental-toughness-for-young-athletes/

Thurott, S. (2023, December 3). *How teen athletes can manage their stress.* Banner Health. https://www.bannerhealth.com/healthcareblog/teach-me/how-teen-athletes-can-manage-their-stress

Trine University. (2021). *Mental toughness: The key to athletic success*. https://www.trine.edu/academics/centers/center-for-sports-studies/blog/2021/mental_toughness_the_key_to_athletic_success.aspx

Trine University. (2023). *The relationship between self-confidence and performance*. https://www.trine.edu/academics/centers/center-for-sports-studies/blog/2023/the_relationship_between_self-confidence_and_performance.aspx

Weinberg, R., Burton, D., Yukelson, D., & Weigand, D. (1993). Goal setting in competitive sport: An exploratory investigation of practices of collegiate athletes. *The Sport Psychologist, 7*(3), 275–289. https://doi.org/10.1123/tsp.7.3.275

Wikman, J. M., Stelter, R., Melzer, M., Hauge, M.-L.T., & Elbe, A.-M. (2014). Effects of goal setting on fear of failure in young elite athletes. *International Journal of Sport and Exercise Psychology, 12*(3), 185–205. https://doi.org/10.1080/1612197x.2014.881070

Wismer, D. (2013, April 1). Tiger Woods: "Winning takes care of everything" (and other quotes of the week). Forbes. https://www.forbes.com/sites/davidwismer/2013/03/31/tiger-woods-winning-takes-care-of-everything-and-other-quotes-of-the-week/

Wong, P. T. (2013, May). *Life is a balancing act*. Dr Paul TP Wong. https://paultpwong.wordpress.com/2013/05/01/life-is-a-balancing-act/

Yates, S. (2024, September 3). BE LIKE MIKE: 23 MICHAEL JORDAN QUOTES THAT PROVE HE'S THE GOAT. REVOLT. https://www.revolt.tv/article/23-michael-jordan-quotes-prove-hes-the-goat

www.ingramcontent.com/pod-product-compliance
Lightning Source LLC
Chambersburg PA
CBHW070434010526
44118CB00014B/2033